Spells and Spooks

Witch Haven Cozy Mystery - book 1

K.E. O'Connor

K.E. O'Connor Books

While every precaution has been taken in the preparation of this book, the publisher assumes no responsibility for errors or omissions, or for damages resulting from the use of the information contained herein.

SPELLS AND SPOOKS

ISBN: 978-1-915378-28-6

Written by: K.E. O'Connor

Preface

The Witch Haven series has been created so you
spend time with four amazing witches:

Books 1-3 tell Indigo's story: Spells and Spooks,
Hexes and Haunts, Curses and Corpses

Books 4-6 tell Luna's story: Muffins and Moonlight,
Cupcakes and Cauldrons, Pancakes and Potions

Book 7-9 tell Odessa's story: Hauntings and High
Jinx, Hauntings and Havoc, Hauntings and Hoaxes

Book 10-12 tell Storm's story: The Case of
the Screaming Skull, The Case of the Poisoned
Pumpkin, The Case of the Cursed Candy

And there are two bonus origin stories to enjoy:
Fire Fang and Silvaria

Chapter 1

I never thought I'd return to the place where I killed sixty-six people.

Every step I took past the wooden Witch Haven village sign felt wrong, and I almost expected an alarm to go off and a spell to toss me back the way I'd come.

I wouldn't have blamed the residents one bit if they'd rigged something up to stop me returning.

Even the path I walked on seemed unwelcoming as I stumbled in a pothole and almost landed on my butt.

There never used to be holes in the paths. This village was making it clear I wasn't welcome home. No surprise there.

It had been fifteen years since I'd crossed the border into the magical community I'd grown up in. I recognized the familiar outlines of some of the ancient cottages and the old, gnarled trees I used to play in. It was as if time had stood still.

Well, almost.

The once welcoming atmosphere Witch Haven was renowned for, radiated with tension and suspicion.

I glanced over my shoulder, convinced I was being followed, but the street was deserted. The tight ache in my shoulders still stuck fast.

When had Witch Haven changed? Had this hopeless atmosphere descended after the killings? I'd not had the option to stick around to see how the village coped with losing so many people in a single day.

A soft sigh slid from my lips. If only they knew just how many had escaped that night, they might have held me a welcome home parade, complete with pitchforks and burning effigies in my image.

What this little place didn't know, was that we'd planned to kill six hundred and sixty-six people. And we'd almost gotten away with it. What's one little missing digit between neighbors?

But I wasn't back to finish what we'd started. My murderous desires had been trained out of me. And I didn't even remember why we started along that path. Some things were best left in the past.

I stopped outside the Fandango bakery with its white and pink paint job, and rested my forehead against the cool glass, peering at the empty shelves that were usually crammed with delicious, sugary treats. I'd spent most of my childhood in this place, feasting on the desserts provided by Luna Brimstone's family.

Not that I'd had a terrible home life and needed the escape, but who could resist the allure of fresh, still warm and gooey bakery goodies? It was teenage girl heaven.

I hadn't spoken to Luna since that fateful, murderous day. It made sense she wouldn't want to stay friends with someone who'd planned to wipe out half the village, Luna's family included.

But even after all this time, I missed our late-night conversations and midnight feasts. And I missed her easy laugh and her warm hugs. Luna was a big hugger. Me, not so much, but I always accepted one from her.

Another sigh came out of me. I couldn't put off the inevitable any longer. I hadn't wanted to come back to Witch Haven, but I'd been given no choice.

I turned away from the bakery, walked past the long curving row of independent stores, from the apothecary to the wand store, and turned down Buttercup Lane. It was a walk I knew only too well.

Darkness closed in on either side as the trees cast their long shadows over the dirt path that led to my stepmom's house. Magda Ash, the woman who'd treated me like her own until the end.

I closed my eyes and kept on walking. I'd snuck along this path so many times late at night after being out past curfew that I really could do it with my eyes closed. I knew every bend, dip, and every spiky bush to avoid. Even after more than a decade away.

Keeping my eyes closed also meant I didn't need to acknowledge the tears that sprung up out of nowhere.

I wasn't sad, though. I was angry. Angry tears were the worst, and I wasn't a pretty crier. I'd never met anyone who could cry and still look cute. That only happened in the movies. No one looked good with swollen eyelids and a soggy nose.

I'd been waiting for this day to come ever since Magda went to prison. It could have been worse. Instead of prison for the rest of her life, she could have been stripped of her powers and sent into the mortal world.

But the authorities had wanted answers from her. They wanted to know the reason we'd committed such awful, unforgiveable crimes.

Magda never talked. She never revealed the truth. And neither did I. There was a good reason for that. I didn't know why we'd done it. I had no memory of that day, or the week leading up to that dark time in Witch Haven's history.

My therapist said it was the shock blocking out traumatic events. It was the brain's way of coping.

I had no idea whether that was true, but her report meant I wasn't constantly questioned by the authorities. The same couldn't be said for my stepmom.

Now, they'd never know the truth. Because Magda was dead, and I was here to deal with the mess she'd left behind.

I stopped at the end of the lane, turned on my heel, and stared at the large, looming detached house in front of me. This had been my home for seventeen years. My biological mom died giving birth to me, and my dad remarried when I was less than a year old. Magda had been an awesome stepmom and had fit right in this house.

My gaze tightened as I scanned the yard. All the flowerbeds at the front were wildly overgrown. It looked like no-one had touched them since Magda's imprisonment. I certainly hadn't, and she hadn't left behind a single friend in the village who'd keep an eye on this place. No one wanted anything to do with a dark-magic-using witch or her crazy stepdaughter.

I pulled a folded letter from the pocket of my long, black coat and unfolded it. It was written on thick cream parchment paper using ink. It was typical of the Magic Council to think it was okay to chop down trees to create such luxurious and wasteful paper. It was their style. They were full of so much pomposity and self-righteousness that it made me queasy.

I'd read this letter a dozen times since it arrived three weeks ago and knew the contents off by heart.

Dear Indigo Ash,

Following the death of your stepmother, Magda Ash, you are required to clear her residence at 354 Buttercup Close in Witch Haven. As you are aware, the property has been left to you in her will.

This property, therefore, falls under your responsibility. As does the following:
- *Thirteen years' of unpaid tax*
- *Death duties*
- *The immediate removal of all illicit magic items*

You have twenty-eight days to pay the money owed and remove the items.

I smirked as I read that line. Every day I'd ignored the letter. Then new letters had arrived. They didn't fly in Hogwarts style by magical owl, but I got a letter through the door every other day, demanding a response.

The Magic Council must be keen on getting Magda's place cleared out, and the money owed them. They'd be lucky to get all their cash back. I had no pot of gold. I scraped by on a pittance, choosing not to use my magic, and worked cash-in-hand jobs whenever I could get them. That meant I had zero savings, and no way of paying the six-figure debt that came with this place.

Not that I wanted anything to do with the house. This was where it all started, the slide into darkness. This was the place where Magda had plotted murder, with me as her willing sidekick.

Each time I'd ignored a letter, the contents became less friendly and more challenging.

What finally prompted me to return was the threat of jail for non-compliance and further re-education to ensure my magic abilities hadn't gone astray.

I grimaced as the memories of my last re-education surfaced. A year in an open prison, working alongside some of the most twisted and meanest magic users I'd ever met. And the Magic Council's version of re-education was to find methods that effectively drained and restrained my magic, so I always felt like a malnourished puppy.

It took them a while to figure out what tamped down my power. Magda had trained me well, and I was competent in all magic use, excelling in elemental magic.

But my time in prison had been a painful daily drag, the food terrible, and the cell sparse and devoid of comfort. Well, it was a prison. I couldn't have expected anything else.

My imprisonment had slowly worn down my resistance until I'd become a pale version of what I once was.

Ash witches had been magnificent. Fire magic was our strength. We were respected in all communities. Known as protectors, fearless, driven, and assured in our use of such potent power.

And Magda had worked with me to stoke my magic and show me how strong I could be.

The Ash witch reputation was now shredded. And all because of me.

Since then, I'd stepped away from magic. Sure, I'd had no choice when I got sent to prison, and I should be grateful that was all I got.

I'd been seventeen when the murders happened, so was tried as a minor. If I'd been a few months older, I'd have gone to the same place as Magda. And look what happened to her. She'd lasted three years in maximum security.

I rested a hand on the gate that led to the overgrown path to the dark purple front door. I tugged a strand of my straggly hair and smiled. Magda had painted that door to match my hair the first time I'd dyed it.

"Stop!" I whispered the word into the cool night air. I had to forget the happy memories, too. There was nothing happy about coming back here. I was here for one reason only.

My plan was simple. Get in, clear out the house, and leave. I'd sell the place for whatever I could get, clear the debts as much as I could, and wipe this miserable mission from my thoughts as soon as I walked past the sign telling me I was leaving Witch Haven.

And I'd arrived in the middle of the night for a good reason. I could work when it was dark without being disturbed, sleep in the day, and avoid seeing anyone.

I reckoned it would take me three days to clear this place, and then I could get out before anyone knew I'd been here. I didn't need to hang around and wait for a sale to go through. A realtor would deal with that. So long as I made it clean enough for viewings and wiped out any dark remnants of my family from the place, I could go back to my life.

It was better that way. No one wanted an Ash witch in this village. And I didn't want to bump into anyone from my past. There'd be no wonderful memories to share with them. Everyone remembered me for one thing. I was a dark witch. A killer.

I shoved the gate open a few inches, its hinges protesting from lack of use. But it wasn't just a rusty hinge making it hard to get in.

My breath caught in my throat. Magda's magic was still alive. She must have warded this place before being arrested. I'd recognize her magic signature anywhere.

My heart gave a painful thud. I missed her magic. It always felt like home and smelled faintly of freshly baked bread. That was until she'd changed.

This magic surrounding the house felt distorted. Of course it would. Magda was dead, so there was nothing keeping the magic refreshed.

"You're not welcome here." I gripped the wound on my hand. If I had my magic, I could have healed the bloody peck in seconds. "This is my home now. Flap off and don't come back." The mean bird didn't need to know this was only my home for a few days.

The crow gave another rusty cackle, before taking to the sky and soaring in an arc around the house.

I kept a close eye on the evil bird as I headed to the porch. I placed one foot on the first step and was suddenly flying through the air. I landed with a thud on my butt by the gate, winded, and a jarring pain radiating up my spine.

"Oh, come on! You must recognize me. I grew up here. You're mine now. I've got the dumb paperwork to prove it." There was no way these wards were keeping me out of this house.

I charged back to the steps and ran my hands over the wards. This magic was much stronger, and not happy to have an intruder on the premises.

Magda must have installed two barriers of protection. The first defense was already eroding, but these were strong, and far more powerful than anything I had in my feeble arsenal. I didn't even have an arsenal, I had a half-empty water pistol that wouldn't shoot straight.

Resentment simmered through me. Stripping a witch of her powers was a humiliation. It sent a message to the world that she couldn't be trusted with her innate ability. She wasn't worthy to keep magic.

It was the Magic Council's way of teaching me a lesson and setting an example to other magic users who broke the rule of using their powers to harm others.

You could legitimately use magic to defend yourself and if you were in danger, but you never maliciously used it to harm innocents. And there'd been plenty of innocents lost the day Magda and I tried to bring down this place.

I sagged against the porch. I was cold, tired, and hungry. I needed sleep, and a good meal. I'd grabbed a sandwich when I'd left my apartment in downtown York Town six hours ago. Now, I regretted not eating properly. And I hadn't even thought about what I'd do for food once I got here. There was no way I was dropping in to the diner to say hello to old friends. They'd probably poison me.

Magda used to keep a supply of tinned food. I hoped it was still there. Tinned goods were just like Twinkies. They lasted forever.

I didn't want to tackle the wards now, but I had no choice, unless I wanted to sleep outside. The longer I delayed, the more likely it was that someone would see me, and rumors spread like dirt on a white dress in this place. Then the trouble really would begin.

I had to stick to my plan. Get in, clear the house, and get out. Avoiding everyone while I did that.

A low growl caught my attention, and my muscles stiffened. I turned toward the sound and spotted two glowing yellow eyes staring at me.

Great, a hungry were-beast thinking I was its next meal. My night had just gone from lousy to a horror show.

Chapter 2

I didn't blink. I didn't want to miss what would come out of the shadows. So I stared and stared. And the yellow eyes stared right back.

If this growling creature was looking for its next meal, it would be disappointed. There wasn't much meat on me. I'd always run skinny and took no pleasure in food these days.

"Go hunt someone else," I muttered to the shadowy thing watching me. "This is my land, and you're trespassing. Don't think I won't fire magic at your furry butt if you stay here much longer."

"If all your magic spells are as pathetic as the one you performed on Crow, then I have nothing to worry about," a deep, throaty voice purred out of the darkness.

Yep, that had to be a were-kitty cat looking for something to play with.

"That thing took me by surprise," I said. "You don't want to make a mistake by crossing me."

"I've crossed you before, Indigo Ash, and I lived to tell the tale."

I tilted my head. "Who are you? Show yourself."

"I'm offended. You really don't remember me?"

"Nope. But then I haven't been around here for a while."

"As everyone is well aware." The eyes blinked, and a second later, a scrawny black cat with the tip missing off its tail appeared.

My jaw dropped. "Nugget! You can't be here."

"I assure you, I am. But I'm much more interested in why you're here. Did they finally let you out?"

I snapped my mouth shut. "You must be at least forty years old."

"And your point?"

"You can't be alive. What exactly are you? Some sort of zombie cat?" He was giving off a ripe odor. Had he been dragged back from the grave by some twisted spell?

"Magda made me her familiar, just before she turned loco. Therefore, I get the luxury of a long life."

"Huh! She never told me that. She always said she'd never pick one familiar because the other animals would get jealous and squeak about favoritism."

He flicked his tail around his paws and settled on the ground. "You were too busy trying to destroy this place to notice. I see your time away from Witch Haven has done you no favors. You've aged much worse than me. What are you now, fifty?"

"Thirty-two!" I glowered at him. "And I never planned on coming back here ever again."

"And yet here you are. You couldn't keep away from the place. You're wasting your time if you're looking for something to fix your magic. Magda's magic was always stronger than yours, but it's warped over time. You should leave while you still can. Nobody wants you here."

I frowned at him. He'd never been this mean. Nugget had been an adorable fluff ball. "I get why most people in the village hate me, but what's your deal? We used to get along."

"Your memory must be as faulty as your spellcasting. I endured you because I had no choice. You were here, and I wanted to be around Magda, so I put up with you."

I shook my head. That wasn't right. All through my childhood, he'd been an awesome cat. Funny, entertaining, and really tolerant of a brat determined to dress him in a cape and mini witch's hat and play zoomies with him in the yard.

A rusty cawing noise came from the roof of the house.

"Is that a friend of yours?" I said.

"Ignore him. Crow's broken."

"Crow? That's his name?"

"That's who he is."

"We should call him Russell. You know, like the actor?"

Nugget sniffed. "You can call him what you like."

"What's his deal?"

"You don't remember Crow?"

"Should I?"

Nugget's narrow-eyed gaze shifted over me. "Perhaps not. It seems the Magic Council has done a number on you. Just how much of your memory did they strip away?"

I shrugged. "You're asking the wrong person. That's the thing with memory removal, it stops you from remembering."

He gave a small snort and licked one paw. "Crow was around during the final six months. He latched onto Magda and tried to be her attack bird. He was always a failure and kept going after the wrong people. He's got some superiority complex and thinks he's an eagle."

Russell made another cawing noise and swept past, dropping something from his claws.

Nugget dodged out the way as stones rained down on him. "No one is impressed, you stupid, feathered freak."

"Hey, Russell, stop attacking me. This is my place now," I said. "You can hang out on the roof if you like, but you're not stopping me from getting inside."

The disgruntled noise Russell made suggested he was unimpressed by that idea. I didn't blame him. I didn't like it either.

I glanced back at the house. "You've stuck around all this time? Ever since Magda got taken?"

"Where else would I go?" Nugget said.

"She's been gone for years. Couldn't you have become someone else's familiar?"

"As if anyone would want me after associating with Magda. I'm an outcast. So is Crow."

"Russell."

"Crow!"

"We'll let him decide," I said. "Crow, Russell is the name of an awesome warrior. He had all the ladies swooning over him and killed a ton of bad guys. It fits your character."

There was silence, then a small caw.

"He loves it. Russell it is," I said.

"You're both idiots," Nugget muttered. "Joining another family wasn't an option. Everyone knew I'd lived here. They think I'm damaged goods."

"You could have tried. It can't have been fun stuck here. Can you get inside?"

Nugget flicked his tail from side to side. "No."

"You've lived out here in all weathers?"

Nugget finished washing his paw. "I have some magic. It sustains me. And Russell... I mean, Crow, keeps me company, even though he annoys me most of the time."

I looked at the wild garden. It gave off a spooky vibe. There'd be no way I'd camp out here.

"I can't say I blame them for having no interest in me," Nugget said. "I didn't see it coming."

I rubbed my forehead, a dull ache forming behind my eyes. "Yeah, neither did I. Now I'm left with Magda's mess to tidy up."

"Why? Has something happened to her?"

"Oh! You don't know."

"Know what?" Nugget stood. "Where is Magda? Are they letting her out? Is she coming home?" His tail flicked over his back.

"Nugget, no. The opposite. I'm so sorry, but she died in prison three months ago." A burst of pain punctured my chest. I shouldn't be sad. When Magda died, she'd been a different person. Not the warm, loving witch who'd raised me.

A weird, choking rattle shot out of Nugget. He dashed away.

"Hey, are you okay?"

17

"I'm fine." His croaky voice came from behind the bush.

I didn't know whether to give him a moment or comfort him. I didn't like this mean, jaded version of Nugget who stank like he'd bathed in a swamp, but he sounded in distress.

I waited another minute. Then he emerged from the bush, his tail swishing from side to side. "I had a hairball. What happened to Magda?"

"Are you sure you're OK?" I wanted to pet him, but didn't want to risk getting slashed.

"Perfect. Magda. What happened to her?"

"I got a report from the prison she was being held in. Apparently, she got her hands on illegal magic and tried to break out. The prison was warded with protective spells, and her magic backfired. It killed her." I cleared my throat. "I never got to see her. They thought it wasn't safe for us to be together."

Nugget hissed and his fur bristled. "You don't think that's suspicious?"

"That my evil, dark magic using stepmom finally had magic go bad on her? Not particularly."

"Magda was a magnificent witch, and your ability paled beside hers."

"I agree. She was awesome."

"And she'd never allow herself to be destroyed by her own spell. How was she when you last saw her?"

"I, um, well, I didn't see her after she went inside. It was one of the conditions from the Magic Council. They forbade us from seeing each other again. They said she was a bad influence." I pressed a hand against my stomach as it churned. Maybe I could have tried harder to visit. I'd started dozens

18

of letters, hoping one of them would get through to her, but hadn't sent a single one.

My hot gaze flicked to the front door. The last time I'd seen Magda was when she was dragged from this house, cursing anyone who got too close, and sending out blasts of damaging magic. Those final memories of her still haunted my dreams.

"You abandoned her," Nugget said.

I sucked in a deep breath. "It seems you aren't listening to me. The Magic Council made it impossible for us to visit each other. Besides, I spent my first year in an open prison being re-educated. When I got out, I had to have weekly sessions with a therapist to make sure I stayed on track. My magic still remains constrained."

"An open prison? You could leave?"

"Under certain conditions. I had a long list of those set against my name. It wasn't worth the hassle."

"You've always been weak," Nugget said. "Some things never change. Did the therapy work out for you?"

"Can't you tell? My life's a dream." I tipped my head forward, tiredness seeping through me. "You know, you don't have to stick around. Magda's not coming back, so there's nothing for you here."

"There's nothing for you, either. And this isn't your home. You gave up on it."

"I had no choice."

"I'm not leaving." Nugget swished his tail.

We stood in silence, angry staring at each other.

Russell cawed a few times.

Nugget blinked first. "If Magda left you this house, that means she left me in your care."

"Nope. Familiars weren't mentioned in her will," I said.

"She may not have used my name specifically, but the intent was there. You get the house, you get everything in it. And that includes me."

"That's not true. And, technically, you're not in the house."

"I'm in the yard. It's the same thing."

My headache intensified. "I can just ignore you. Besides, there's no point in getting friendly, I'm only going to be here a few days."

Nugget slumped onto the ground and huffed out a breath. He looked as defeated as I felt. He was a sorry looking cat. I remember him as a huge, sleek, handsome black fluff ball, with a bushy tail and sparkling amber eyes. He was a shadow of his once handsome, fluffy self. Dark magic had done a number on both of us.

"You can hang out here while I clear out the house, but that's it. I'm not staying, and I'm not taking you with me when I go," I said.

"I wouldn't come with you even if you begged me to."

"You're welcome," I said.

"You're not." Nugget dragged himself to his paws. "But I'll stay for now. Inside, there's a supply of cat food. That's mine."

"Then we have a problem. To get to the cat food, we have to break through these wards." I hovered a finger over the barrier preventing me from getting to the door.

"You won't be able to do that with what's left of your magic," Nugget said. "You should give up. Go home."

The scruffy, mean cat was shouting my own feelings at me. Nugget was bitter and broken and clearly didn't think anything of me. But why should he? I'd helped Magda destroy this village, and rip apart friendships and bonds that had been there for generations.

Ever since that day, I'd cut connections with anyone. I didn't do companions or friends, and I'd never had a familiar.

A witch without a familiar was an oddity. But I was better off alone. If I was on my own, I couldn't hurt anyone.

It seemed Nugget thought the exact same thing if his unfriendly welcome was anything to go by.

"There has to be a way in," I said.

"Find it." He sighed and sank onto his belly again.

I kneeled beside him. I hated seeing any animal unhappy, even if he was a huge fluffy ball of snark. "I could always look for a new home for you."

He growled at me. "If you take me to the animal rescue place, I'll kill you."

"You can try, fluff ball." I stood and pressed my hands against the wards. They pulsed a warning beneath my fingers. I decided not to push any harder, or I'd get shoved away again, and my spine was still groaning.

I yelped and leaped out the way as something slashed across the back of my ankle. I turned to see Nugget with a raised paw, ready to strike again.

21

"What's wrong with you?" I rubbed the gashes on my leg. His claws had gone straight through my black leggings.

"I told you to leave."

"And I told you this house is mine. Clear out."

"I'm going nowhere. If you don't like me being here, you go." Nugget hissed in despair, his fur puffed up. "Leave. Now."

"Make me, fuzzy face."

A harsh cawing came from over my head, and Russell swooped down and dive-bombed Nugget.

Nugget slashed the air, trying to reach the crow. "Attack her! She's the enemy. We don't want her here. She left us. Peck her."

My heart stuttered. Nugget was angry because I left?

Russell wheeled around and dived at Nugget again.

At least I had one ally. Not that I needed one, but it was nice that Nugget's claws were no longer aimed in my direction. Although he had a right to be hissy. I'd stayed away for too long.

I dodged out the way as Russell circled back for another dive, not entirely convinced he wouldn't change sides.

Nugget turned tail and raced into the bushes.

Russell gave a loud cackle of success as he swooped past me, dipping one wing as he did so.

"I was handling myself just fine, but thanks for the backup," I said.

Something tapped on the back of my hand.

I looked down, and my eyes widened. A huge black spider with long spindly legs sat on my thigh.

"I, um, hi? Please don't tell me you're venomous and also hate me. I've had enough crud to deal with today."

The spider tapped my hand again.

Okay, so it wasn't biting me. That was a positive start. "You're scarily impressive, but I still don't want those fangs sunk into my hand. Is there something I can do for you?"

The spider waved two long legs at me.

I held out a finger, and we made contact. The second we did, a sliver of power shot through me, leaving me shaking. "Whoa! You're stronger than you look."

"As are you. I sense your power is restrained, but if we work together, combine our strengths, we can get into the house." The spider's voice was feminine and there was a slight crackly undertone. This was definitely more than your average large, hairy house spider.

"Thanks for the offer, but I'm good. I'll figure out a way through these wards."

"Magda's wards are unstable. They haven't been repaired for many years, and no one has been by to strengthen them. They're not safe. If you deactivate them on your own, you could die."

"It won't be that dangerous. And I really don't need anyone's help."

The spider waggled a leg as if telling me off. "There's no shame in asking for help, especially when you've been incapacitated by others."

"I'm not incapacitated. I still have magic."

"You have some ability, but you're weak. What's inside that house will make you strong, but you can't do it alone. Have you ever heard the phrase there's no I in team?"

I gritted my teeth. I'd had this kind of skull numbing talk from my therapist. "That's true. But technically, there's a me. And there's no u. And there are three i's in individual."

The spider rubbed her fangs together, as if considering sinking them into my fleshy palm. "You always had a smart mouth."

"Um... we've met before?"

"We have. Now, stop being stubborn, and let's figure this out together."

I sighed. I was exhausted and hungry. I just wanted a sit down, something hot to drink, and an hour to snooze. But I was only accepting this one favor. I wasn't working with the familiars Magda had left behind. I didn't need any complications, nothing that would tie me here. I had enough smudges on my soul to last me several broken lifetimes. Becoming a part of Witch Haven again wasn't an option.

"Do you have a name?" I asked.

"I'm Hilda."

Someone clearing their throat by the gate had me turning. I narrowed my eyes and my stomach clenched. As if this night couldn't get any worse. I'd recognize someone who worked for the Magic Council anywhere.

A tall, broad-shouldered guy wearing a wide, broad-brimmed hat, glared at me. "You're finally home, Indigo."

Chapter 3

"If you take one more step, you'll be trespassing on my land. That gives me rights." I stared down the sharp-faced guy. He was tall, dark and stubbled. And I wanted him gone.

"That sounds like a threat," he said. "You don't have time to make those, not if you want to clear out your stepmom's things."

"You're here to check up on me? Or are you hoping to find some of Magda's magic to take away for the council to exploit?"

"How do you know I work at the Magic Council?"

"They have a type. You're it."

He shrugged. "Nothing that twisted witch left behind interests us."

I slid my tongue over my teeth. "Who are you?"

"Olympus Duke."

A shiver of surprise ran through me. I'd heard that name plenty of times, but had never met the head of the Magic Council before. He rarely made public appearances. He was more myth than real. I must be in trouble if he was on my doorstep checking me out.

A thin smile crossed his lips. "I see you've heard of me."

"Can't say I have. What are you doing hanging around my old home?"

"I'm here to give you this." He drew a sheet of paper from his inside jacket pocket and held it out.

I knew better than to take anything from a member of the Magic Council without learning what it was. "Is that another order to send me back to prison? You can't do that. I've done nothing wrong. I'm here because you insisted I come."

"Providing you pay the debts listed on this docket, you won't go back to prison."

"You're out of luck if you think you're getting all that money out of me. I've got nothing."

His dark gaze lifted to the house. "That's not strictly true."

"You strike out again. Even after I've sold it, I'll probably still owe money."

"Then give me something else." Olympus extended his hand, and a coil of magic spun from his palm. It looped around me and tightened against my throat.

I grabbed the magic, fighting to get free from its fierce hold as it stung my skin like lemon juice in an open wound.

Russell and Nugget stood to one side, and what may have been anxiety marred their faces. Nope, they weren't worried. They didn't care about me. Hilda had vanished.

I dropped to my knees as the remains of my magic drained from me. It was only when black spots appeared in my vision, that Olympus withdrew his magic bind.

He shook out his hands. "Your re-education appears to have been successful. I expected to obtain more from you."

"Go away! Nobody likes a magic leech." I pulled myself upright, my throat burning and my insides shaking.

"You had nothing else to offer. Call that a partial payment for this debt." He waved the paper at me.

"That's all you're getting," I said. "You need to leave."

Olympus didn't move, just stood there looking smug and tall and annoying. "Or what? I don't see a queue of long-lost friends waiting to welcome you home. There's no one to help you get rid of me."

"That's only because they don't know I'm here."

He arched a brow. "And why is that? Why didn't you let your friends know you were returning home?"

"As if you can't guess, wise guy." I jerked my chin up. "Was there something else you needed?"

Olympus' gaze ran over me. "Don't linger in this place, Indigo. You're all alone and have no one to protect you. A lone witch is vulnerable to unpleasant things, especially a witch as hated as you."

"I had no plans to stay. But thanks to your buddies at the Magic Council, I had no choice. I'll get what magic items I need, sell this place, and forget I ever lived here."

"That's not acceptable."

I raised my hands to the sky. "Then you guys have your wires crossed. I was ordered back here. What do you expect me to do with the place?"

"Once you break the wards, the house and its toxic power will be destroyed. That's why I'm here, to ensure it happens," Olympus said.

Nugget hissed softly, and his eyes narrowed.

I looked at the building that housed so many happy memories. My gut cramped at the thought of it gone. I should be glad it was about to be destroyed, but this had once been an amazing home. Things had only turned rotten at the end.

I clenched my fists. This was my house. I should be the one who decided if it stayed exactly as it was or was pulled to the ground.

I turned back to Olympus. "You're making a mistake."

"There's no mistake. The Magic Council has decided to wipe this place from history."

"Then they're as stupid as they are inefficient. You may want to take down the house, but you can't erase everyone's memory. There are people living here who remember what happened."

Olympus scrubbed a hand against his chin. "Those with long memories won't last forever. Witch Haven doesn't want this dark stain lingering. We plan to remove all evidence that Magda Ash ever lived here."

"Not yet, you're not." I drew back my shoulders. I may be a powerless witch with no friends, no money, and no prospects, but I had this house. I was only letting it go when I decided it was the right time. "This is my home, and I've got the paperwork to prove it. Magda left this to me. You don't get to decide what happens to it."

"That's where you're wrong. With the debts you've accrued, and your inability to pay them, this can be seized as an asset."

"I'll pay the debts. Once I've sold this place, I should have enough to clear what you're owed." I hoped I'd have enough, but there was no guarantee.

"Why would anyone buy a residence with such a dark past?" Olympus said. "The only people who'll view this place are those with a taste for the macabre. I suppose you could let it out to ghost hunting parties. They may try to conjure the evil spirit of your stepmom."

"They wouldn't dare," I said through gritted teeth. "And I'm not turning my home into a playground for weirdos."

He was silent for a few seconds. "What will you do if you can't sell?"

"You let me worry about that." It had once been a beautiful home and stood on a great plot in a secluded part of the village. Someone would be interested in buying it. Most likely someone who didn't do the proper background checks. Even if I didn't secure the market rate, I'd get something, and get the Magic Council off my back.

"The clock is ticking," Olympus said. "These debts need to be repaid quickly."

"I know! That's why I'm here. You lecturing me is only slowing me down."

Olympus took a step closer, hovering right by the gate.

Russell took off, squawking, and circled around his head. His talons stretched out as he swooped lower.

Olympus blasted out magic, almost hitting Russell. "Keep your tainted familiars away from me."

"They're not mine. I don't have familiars."

Nugget muttered something under his breath I didn't catch. It was probably rude.

Russell circled again and fired something out of his beak. It landed with a sloppy plop on Olympus's expensive long black coat and slid down the arm.

I stifled a laugh as Olympus scowled at the mess. "It's time you left. I have no control over these animals, but they clearly have good taste since they don't like you."

He tossed the papers on the ground. "Don't be late repaying your debt. The interest grows daily."

"As soon as I have any money, you'll be added to the long list of those who'll get some." I left the papers where they were. If they blew away, I could claim I'd never been given them and didn't know the debt existed. It wasn't a mature move, but I was tired and hurting from being drained of my magic.

Olympus frowned at me. "And since you can't be trusted, I have backup to keep an eye on you." He clicked his fingers, and a few seconds later, two large leather-clad trolls stomped into view.

I tipped back on my heels. They were over seven feet tall, broad, with tough gray skin and pudgy faces. "I don't need babysitting. I have no plans to misbehave."

"None of us realized Magda's plans until the two of you attempted to annihilate this village," Olympus said. "We need to make sure you don't try anything like that again."

"For the love of all things broomstick, I've served my time. I've been re-educated. And as you felt when you rudely invaded my magic reserves, I've barely any magic left. I can't even conjure a simple light spell anymore. I'm barely a witch."

"It still doesn't make you safe to be around," Olympus said. "The trolls are here to ensure you maintain order. And they'll remain here until you leave."

The trolls glared at me.

I had no problems with trolls. They could be quick to anger and used their fists before thinking, but so long as you stayed out of their way and didn't rile them up, you were fine. But these two looked like they wanted to kill me. They must know my history. If I tangled with them, I'd be lucky to get out of here with all my limbs still attached to my body.

"Let me know if she causes trouble," Olympus said to the trolls. He turned toward the village.

"Oh! You're leaving so soon? I was about to invite you in for a cup of tea and ask about your day."

Olympus jabbed a finger at the papers that fluttered in the wind. "Pay your debts and leave Witch Haven." He walked away.

I didn't move as I watched the trolls settle into place by the gate. I huffed out a breath and stamped on a sheet of paper that floated past. I hadn't wanted to come back to Witch Haven, yet Olympus made it sound like I was being deliberately nefarious, and only back to cause trouble. I'd been living a quiet life, skimming so far below the radar that I wasn't even a blip on anyone's screen. It was the Magic Council who'd dragged me here thanks to their demanding letters and insistence I repay debts that had nothing to do with me.

Hilda clambered up my arm and stopped on my shoulder. She dabbed one long leg against my cheek. "Are you ready to work together now?"

"I don't have a choice. Thanks to that jerk, I'm so tired I can barely keep my eyes open. Doing magic on my own is impossible."

"I knew you'd see sense and realize you need us."

"I never said I needed you. I don't need anybody."

"We all need friends."

I blinked my gritty eyes. Was that true? I'd been friendless for such a long time, that it felt natural.

A soft laugh came out of the spider. "Now, how about we work together, crack these wards open, and get inside? I've never liked the smell of trolls. They remind me of sweating mushrooms, all mossy and earthy."

I glanced back at the trolls, who had their backs to me. "Fine. But this doesn't mean we're a team. I don't play well with others."

"It's good to be independent." Hilda waggled her legs at Nugget and Russell. "Come join in the fun, you two. It's time we got inside."

Russell soared over my head, and I flinched as he settled on my shoulder, expecting another painful jab from his beak.

"If you peck me, you'll be my next meal," I said.

He shuffled from foot to foot and fluttered his wings.

"Let's all get along," Hilda said. "Everyone's tired and cold, but there's no need to be mean. Open your magic and let's join together."

I had barely any magic to offer, but threw out what I had. Russell opened his wings and a blast of silvery gray magic shot into the wards, mingling with my own pathetic pale pink flow.

Nugget muttered and grumbled, before adding his own magic to the mix. It was orange and had jagged sparkles running through it.

I was most surprised by Hilda's magic. It blasted out of her fangs in an impressive rainbow arc, twirling and spiraling round the rest of our spells, before punching into the wards. It felt more like dragon magic than arachnid power, but I'd take it.

After several minutes of pulsing magic, the wards wavered, bending beneath the combined power of our spells.

Sweat slid down my cheek and my arms shook. I was out of practice when it came to using magic. I barely used it from one month to the next, and thanks to Olympus, my depleted, rusty reserves were exhausted.

"Keep going," Hilda said. "The wards are bending. We're almost in."

"I can smell the cat food from here," Nugget said.

I concentrated and gave it everything I could. There was a blast of light, and the wards crashed down. Magda's magic seeped across the yard in a silver river and trickled away.

I staggered to one side, making Russell alarm call and fly off.

"Steady now," Hilda said. "Magda left behind strong magic to protect your home. It may not be the only thing in this house you need to be careful of."

"I hope it is. I've had enough surprises for one night." I staggered up the porch steps and shoved open the door.

I leaned against the frame as my gaze flicked around the hallway with its sage green walls, bunches of dried herbs, and exposed floorboards.

A sigh of exhaustion slid from my lips. Home sour home.

Chapter 4

I hadn't expected to feel anything when I walked through the door of my old home again. I'd been away for so long that most of my childhood memories were blurry and indistinct.

But my heart raced and tears blurred my vision as I looked around the living room, the memories punching into me like jackhammers. There was the old yellow chair by the open fireplace Magda used to sit in and read to me. There was the wonky, handcrafted wooden seat I'd used when I was younger to sit at the table and eat my meals.

I could just see a glimpse of the oak work surfaces in the kitchen where I'd spent hours brewing spells alongside Magda. She'd always sing when we worked on our spells, old tunes about forest witches and love.

I had a terrible singing voice and sounded like an angry tomcat with a sore throat. But she never complained when I joined in, getting the words wrong and missing the right key.

Nugget barged past me. "This place is a dump."

Russell swooped in over my head and settled on a cobweb covered wooden branch in the corner of the room.

I looked around again, shaking off the memories flooding my thoughts. Nugget had a point about the state of the place. Dust covered every surface, and furniture was overturned, capturing the day the Magic Council had burst in and grabbed Magda and me. It was like a time capsule of the worst moment of our lives. The day everything was turned upside down.

There was no point in having a pity party. I needed to get on and clear out anything useful, then I had to get this place on the market.

Despite what Olympus said, this house would sell. It was a quirky house with a ton of character. Someone would want it. They had to. I needed them to buy it. The option of me staying here wasn't one to dwell on. There was no home for me in Witch Haven.

Hilda tapped the back of my hand. "Is it good to be home?"

"This hasn't been my home for a long while." I glanced down at the spider. "Did you choose to live here?"

"I did. We all did. It was a happy home."

"My bedding is moldy. It needs airing." Nugget sat on a pile of old towels in the corner of the room.

"Then find a better place to sleep," I said. "Maybe sleep outside since that's what you're used to."

"I'm staying here," he grumbled. "Go find me food."

"Go find a mouse. There'll be huge families of them living in the cupboards."

"I don't catch mice!"

"And I'm not your server for the evening."

We had another glaring competition. Nugget won this time.

I'd just wandered into the kitchen, my hunger making me beyond irritable, when the front door blasted open.

I rushed out to find the trolls standing in the middle of the living room. "What are you doing? I didn't invite you in."

"The boss said we have to take out the junk." The larger of the two trolls made a grab for the yellow chair.

I ran at him and smacked his hands until he dropped the chair. "Leave it! That's not yours. I get to decide what's junk and what stays. All this is mine until I say otherwise."

He shrugged. "The boss said it's got to go."

"Your boss is a smug jerk who doesn't know what he's talking about." The next time I saw Olympus, we'd be having words. Mainly cuss words.

The troll grunted as he looked around. "It's a mess in here. You won't be able to clear this on your own."

"Yes, I will. I don't need help from the Magic Council." I pointed at the door. "You two stick to watching my every move, but keep your hands off my things. And do it outside, so you aren't in the way."

The other troll made a grab for another piece of furniture.

My hand landed on one of Magda's broomsticks and a wave of familiar magic ran through me, making my skin tingle. Before I realized what I was doing, a blast of magic slammed into the troll.

"What the..." He staggered away, rubbing his arm where the magic had whacked him.

I stared at my hands, not sure of the spell I'd used. I had to bluster this out, or the trolls would get mean. "That's your final warning. Get out of my house, or I'll do much worse to you. Don't you know I'm the dark witch's apprentice? I eat trolls for breakfast."

They looked at each other, confusion clear on their squishy faces.

"He said you didn't have magic." The troll who'd been whacked with the spell backed away. "That really stung."

"Olympus doesn't know everything." I glared at the other troll. "Do you want a piece of me, too?"

He shook his head, and they lumbered out.

I ran over and slammed the door shut. I stared at my tingling fingers, stunned into silence by what just happened. I couldn't do magic like that. It was impossible.

"Well, you are full of surprises," Nugget said. "Where have you been hiding that power? You barely made any effort when we were getting through the wards."

I stared at the broomstick leaning against the wall. "From that, I think." Had Magda infused items with her power before being taken? I shook my head. No, it had to be a fluke. But even if I had untapped power left, I had no plans to use it. I'd seen first-hand what having too much magic led to. And even if Magda had left secrets behind before she'd been arrested, I wasn't here for that. This was a last farewell to a place I no longer considered home.

"I'm still hungry," Nugget said.

"And I'm sure there are still mice lurking in the cupboards." I turned away from the broomstick.

Hilda, who was now riding around on my shoulder, tapped my cheek. "Manners cost nothing."

"They do with Nugget. How do you put up with him?"

She jabbed me harder.

I groaned. "Fine. Let's see what's edible."

After a few minutes searching in the kitchen cupboards, I produced a dozen tins of food, mainly vegetables and a few tins of beans, several tins of tuna, and some cat food.

Nugget danced around my legs, twirling his tail around my calf and purring.

"I'll know how to win you over in the future." I opened a tin of cat food and dumped it onto a plate, before putting it on the floor.

His purring intensified as he gobbled it down.

I glanced at Russell. "What do you eat?"

"He likes fruit. And insects. Small mammals if you've got any to hand," Hilda said.

"What about you? Would Russell ever try to eat you?"

Hilda backed up several steps and rubbed her fangs together. "He tried once. He won't ever do it

39

again. That bald patch on his head didn't get there by accident."

I grinned. Hilda was a tough old spider. I opened a can of tinned peaches and left some on the countertop for Russell to eat.

"What about you, Hilda? What's your food of choice?"

"There are plenty of insects in here to keep me full. I like to graze."

"Then we're all sorted with our gourmet meals." I grabbed a tin of beans, a fork from the drawer, and sank into a dusty chair. I couldn't have dreamt up a weirder homecoming if I'd tried.

I jerked upright as something clanged on the floor by the chair. I was cold and stiff from falling asleep after my less than hearty meal of tinned butter beans served from the tin.

I tensed and remained in the seat, firing up what little magic I'd regenerated from my nap. It wasn't the can falling to the floor that had woken me. Someone was inside the house.

There were a few seconds of silence, before soft footsteps on the creaking floorboards began again.

I eased out of the chair, keeping my feeble magic poised on my fingertips.

As the intruder rounded the corner into the living room, I pounced and grabbed them in a headlock.

There was a scream, and nails dug into my forearm.

I let go and backed away as my nose flooded with the familiar smell of cedar wood and raspberry jam tarts. There was only one person I knew who smelled like that.

I grabbed the candlestick off the shelf and sparked a flame against its dusty wick. As it flickered grudgingly to life, I thrust out the candle.

My heart thudded to a stop. "Luna!"

A smile crossed Luna Brimstone's face. "Hey, Indigo! Why did you attack me?"

"I didn't know I was attacking *you*. All I knew was someone had broken into the house and was coming after me."

Luna laughed. "No one's coming after you. I wanted to make sure the rumors were true. You'. really back?" The last time I'd seen her, we'd been seventeen and wide-eyed innocents when it came to magic. Well, sort of innocent. We were teenage girls and always found a little trouble to get into.

Luna was curvier now, her dark hair longer and straighter, and the once thick, dark eyeliner had gone. She'd grown into a striking-looking woman with a wide mouth and intelligent eyes.

I grinned and was about to step forward to hug her, when I froze. Luna wouldn't want anything to do with me. She must hate me. She'd lost her aunt when Magda and I had gone on our rampage.

There were several seconds when we just stared at each other. Why was she here?

"First things first. Let's fix your dismal light situation." Luna walked over to the light switch and tried it.

41

"It won't work. The power's been disconnected," I said. "No one's been here for years, so the bills haven't been paid."

"I can solve that." Luna blasted out a scatter spell, which latched onto the candles in the room and brought them to life. A moment later, we were standing in a warm, welcoming glow.

Luna smiled at me again, a hint of nerves around the edges of her expression. "You should have said you were coming home."

"Why?" I winced, not meaning to sound so sharp.

She jerked her head back and chewed on her bottom lip. "Because I've missed you."

I placed the candle back on the mantelpiece, giving myself a moment to gather my thoughts. I'd taken away one of her family members. She shouldn't have missed me. Luna had every right to be raging mad with me.

I glanced back at her. Was this a ruse? Maybe she was here to kill me.

I ran my tongue over my bottom lip. I wouldn't stop her if she did. It was no less than I deserved.

"Hey! Indigo, talk to me. Why the silent treatment? I really missed you not being around. I reached out a few times to see if you wanted a friend to talk to, but you never replied."

I turned to face her. "We haven't spoken since I left Witch Haven." The sadness in her eyes made my heart ache. There was no anger there, and no hint of vengeance. Had Luna really forgiven me? I don't think I'd be so open-hearted if someone killed a member of my family.

"No, we haven't talked, but I wrote to you." Luna lifted one shoulder, her fingers playing with the hem of her orange tunic. "Not at first. It took everyone a while to piece together what happened here, but I didn't want to lose you as a friend. After a couple of months, I found out where you were and sent you letters."

"You did?" I didn't hide my surprise.

"Sure. I wrote twice a month for six months, but you never got back to me."

"Oh! I never got any of those letters." The prison must have stopped them from getting through. And I'd never once questioned why my friends had dropped me. I didn't have to.

A smile crossed her face. "You didn't? That's good news. I figured you wanted nothing to do with me."

A laugh shot out of me. "And they say I'm the crazy one. Don't you remember what I did?"

"Of course. But you're not crazy." Her gaze cut around the room. "I... I don't blame you."

"You should. I'm not innocent."

"You were a kid back then. You didn't know what you were doing."

"I was seventeen. I had a pretty good idea what was going on."

Luna looked away. "I mean; it was mainly your stepmom. She made you do it, didn't she?"

I scrubbed a finger across my forehead. "Honestly, I don't remember if I was forced into doing anything against my will."

"I'm certain you were. It was a mistake. And magic is hard to control. I've made my fair share of mistakes over the years with spells."

43

"I bet your mistakes didn't kill people."

"I've come close. I work full-time with my uncle in the bakery, and I'm sure I've given lots of people food poisoning. I'm not a natural baker."

"I didn't know you worked there. You always wanted to teach. What happened to that idea?"

"I hadn't planned to go into the family business, but after my aunt... well, you know what happened to her. My uncle wasn't doing so well on his own, so I stayed to help. I only planned on being there for a couple of years, but here I am, over a decade later. I like it. And the free food at the end of the day is always great. Although not for my waistline." Luna patted her stomach.

I clenched my teeth. Talk about derailing your best friend's future. I still couldn't figure out why she wasn't swinging an ax at my head. "You look great. I'm glad things worked out for you."

"I have no complaints." Luna looked around the room again. "This place hasn't changed."

"There's been no-one here to make any changes."

She nodded. "I walk past here sometimes. It's silly, but I sort of hoped I'd see you back fixing up the place. I'd close my eyes and wish you were here."

My heart beat an unsteady rhythm as I sorted through my messy emotions. "Luna, I never meant for your aunt to get caught up in what happened. We... we didn't have any real targets that day. We just..." How could I finish that sentence? We went on a dark magic rampage for fun? We lost control? We didn't care who got hurt, so long as we did maximum damage? Someone go build up the witch bonfire now. I'd throw myself on it.

"You don't have to explain. People gossiped about you and Magda for a long time, but I didn't listen to any of it. I always defended you when they said you were broken and as bad as Magda."

"Magda wasn't bad. She was..." I had nothing. I didn't know what had changed my stepmom and how she'd gotten tangled in dark magic. Maybe she'd simply lost control, used the wrong spell, and it destroyed her. I'd never know for sure what turned her.

I so badly wanted to hug Luna, but kept my hands by my sides. I had to remember, I wasn't here to rekindle friendships. There'd be no point getting to know Luna all over again, especially since I was leaving in a few days.

Luna hummed under her breath and nodded. "Anyway, I couldn't believe it when I heard you were back in the village."

"It didn't take long for the rumor mill to start churning. Who told you I was here?"

"Several people. Olympus Duke has a room in the inn, and he was talking about you when he went to the bar. My uncle heard the news from Bronwyn and then came to tell me."

I tutted. Olympus couldn't resist stirring up trouble for me. He probably hoped the villagers would do his job for him and run me out of this house.

"He paid me an unwelcome visit a few hours ago, telling me what I shouldn't do while I'm here. The bottom line is the Magic Council want me gone as soon as possible."

"I'm not sure I like Olympus," Luna said. "He's too arrogant for my liking. He knows he's good-looking and thinks everyone will be charmed by him. But he's too puffed up with his own authority to be considered yummy."

"Yummy?" I smiled. That was how Luna had always described guys who made her weak at the knees. "I didn't notice he was good-looking. I was too busy being drained."

She gasped. "Drained? He took your magic?"

"What was left of it. He's a jerk."

"If he does that to witches, then I agree with you. Are the trolls outside his?" Luna said.

"Yes. How did you get past them?"

"They didn't stop me from coming in. I told them I was here to see you, and they grunted and waved me by."

"I had to kick them out of here because they started trying to move the junk as they called it. Most of this stuff may be junk, but that's for me to decide." I looked at the dusty furniture, piles of spell books, and knick-knacks on the mantelpiece. It would be easier to light a literal fire and walk away.

"You must have plans to stay for a while if you're fixing up this place," Luna said.

"Um... I haven't decided what to do with the house. There's lots to think about."

"Well, I'm glad you're back. I came as soon as I heard you were home. We should catch up. Have a girls' night."

Sadness settled over me like a smoke clogged cloak. "Luna, I'm not... home. Not really. And I'm amazed you came here. After everything that happened."

"Don't be. I wanted to see my best friend again."

I blinked away tears. "I didn't think we were friends."

"We are. I promise."

"Are you sure you didn't just come to get some gossip to spread around?"

"Hey! That's not fair. I'm not a gossip."

"You always were a bit of a gossip."

She laughed. "Okay, but not about this. And never about you. Friends don't do that to each other."

"I'm glad to hear it." I had to take Luna at her word. She wasn't yelling or blasting spells at me, so I was happy. "It's great to see you."

Luna ran a finger through some dust on a shelf. "I... um, actually, there is more than one reason I came to see you. There's something I need your help with."

I shook my head. Here it was, the kicker. I knew she wasn't here to rekindle a friendship. "You've come to the wrong place if you need help."

"It's your magic. Your skills in a certain area."

"I'm still no good to you. My magic is broken, and the Magic Council is watching me like pompous hawks, just waiting for me to put a foot wrong."

Luna rushed forward and grabbed my hands. "Indigo, I can't do this without you. I need you by my side." Anguish simmered in her eyes as she gripped my hands.

"Why? What's the matter?"

"It's my apartment. It's haunted."

I tilted my head. "Ghosts aren't usually a problem for you. We've always been around them." Magic attracted ghosts. Everyone knew that.

"I don't usually mind the spirits hanging about, but not this one."

"Is he creeping on you when you're in the shower? Banish him if that's the problem." My smile faded. Luna wasn't laughing.

Tears filled her eyes. "It's not that. He wants me dead."

Chapter 5

"Wait! A ghost is trying to kill you?" I wasn't sure I believed Luna. She'd always had an overactive imagination when we'd been kids, but there was no humor on her face as she stared at me. The one emotion I saw was fear. She was terrified.

"I'm certain this ghost has plans to hurt me. And it's been going on for a while. Well, the apartment has always been a little haunted, but those ghosts never caused me trouble. This one is different. And he's chased the others away. He doesn't like to share."

"Where are you living?" The last time I'd seen Luna, she'd been with her aunt and uncle in the apartment above the bakery.

"I've got my own place on Cedar Lane. I fell in love with it the second I stepped through the door. It's got two bedrooms, enormous windows that let in loads of light, and an amazing kitchen so I can work on improving my baking. I have to practice loads to create great desserts."

"You bought it even though you knew it had ghosts?" Ghosts weren't unusual in Witch Haven, but I'd hesitate before buying a place that came with its own resident specter.

"They were friendly. And I didn't buy the place, I'm just renting. When I looked around, one ghost even opened the doors for me, so I had no worries. Then everything changed."

I led Luna to a chair, and we both sat. "Why do you think this ghost is a threat to you?"

Luna pushed up the sleeves of her flower spotted orange tunic to reveal bruises on her arms that looked like large fingerprints.

"Holy broomsticks! A ghost did that to you?"

She nodded. "I was asleep when it happened. I woke to an icy bedroom and two red eyes glowing at me. I couldn't move my arms. That's when I screamed. The ghost laughed and faded away. That was the first time I felt in real trouble. Since then, it's only gotten worse."

"Then move out! Get this ghost out of your life."

"It's my home. I won't be driven out by an angry ghost with an attitude. And I was there first, probably. I want him gone." She leaned over and squeezed my arm. "Indigo, you were always great with ghosts when we were younger."

"Uh, back then I was, but not anymore. I haven't spoken to a ghost in a long time." I still saw plenty of them, and I'd always had an affinity with spirits. Most of the time, they simply wanted to hang out in places they were familiar with, but you occasionally got a ghost who needed reminding he was no longer in the land of the living and to stop causing trouble.

"I know you can help me. When I heard you were back, I had to come and see you, convince you to take a look. You'll figure out what this ghost wants and how to get rid of him."

I hated that Luna was at risk from this ghost. It wasn't fair her life was being ruined because she had an unwelcome house guest. If things were different, I wouldn't hesitate in helping.

"Visit for an hour and take a look around. Maybe you'll pick up something I've missed. I've tried all kinds of spells and even tried to negotiate with this ghost to see if I can convince him to leave. He's not interested. Just yesterday, I came home from the bakery, to find the walls in the living room dripping with slime. And it stank."

"It sounds like you need an exorcism," I said.

"I've tried that. And I've asked around to see what other people think, but no one knows what it is. I've had six different magic users in my place, and they assured me they'd get rid of the ghost. One of them ran out screaming after she was attacked." Luna shook her head, her shoulders slumping. "I'm beginning to think I will have to move out, but I love the place so much. It's not fair my life gets tipped upside down because of a ghost with issues."

"You should move out. It would be simpler and safer for you."

"And let the ghost win! He's nasty. Bullies should never be allowed to prosper." She tugged my arm. "You're here! You can deal with this ghost. It's as if you were sent to help me in my hour of need."

I was no one's savior. And even though a part of me wanted to help Luna, I didn't have my abilities intact. I'd only be a massive burden to her and mess things up even more.

"I'll pay you if that's the problem," Luna said. "I don't make a huge amount of money at the bakery, but I do okay. I have some savings. What do you need?"

I raised a hand. "It's not that. I'd never take your money. But the last thing you need is me back in your life."

"It's exactly what I need. My old friend back. If we work together, we can drive this ghost away and be eating cupcakes for brunch."

"I'm bad news, Luna. My magic is wonky, and everyone who lives here hates me. If they find out I'm trying to fix your ghost problem, things could turn bad for you."

"The villagers don't hate you. They'll be as thrilled as me to know you're back."

Something huge and orange smashed through the living room window and rolled over. It stopped by my feet. It was a pumpkin with the word *killer* etched into it.

I arched an eyebrow and kicked the pumpkin away. "Are you sure about that? Or is this just a weird welcome home gift?"

Luna's mouth hung open. She turned and raced to the window.

I joined her and saw a group of teenagers racing away from the house. "You see. That's not exactly a welcoming party. I should put the wards back up. Trust me, people throwing pumpkins through my window will be the least bad thing to happen if I stay too long."

"It was just teenagers in high spirits. They probably heard the gossip about you and wanted to see if it was true."

"That's not reassuring. Kids getting egged on by their parents gossiping about the arrival of the killer Ash witch. It'll only get worse." My gaze shifted to the trolls, who seemed to be asleep upright. That was a nifty skill to have. "Let's go see why my guards did nothing to stop the vandalism."

"Maybe you shouldn't bother them. They were surly with me, even though I gave them my best smile."

"What's the point of having them guarding my home if they don't stop this kind of thing from happening?"

Luna hurried along beside me as I headed outside and over to the trolls.

"Hey! Why didn't you stop that mob from smashing my window?" I yelled.

The trolls didn't even look at me.

"Why would we do that?" Burly troll number one finally said.

"Because someone could have been hurt. There's glass everywhere."

He grunted. "We're here to protect the village and everyone who lives in it from you, not you or your house."

A flare of indignation made my cheeks burn. "Then you're in for a boring time. I have no plans to do anything bad while I'm here." Although I was tempted to do something horrible to these trolls. I could spike their coffee with laxatives, or think terrible things about them. Yes, that was about the extent of my powers.

"Let's forget about it." Luna tugged gently on my arm. "And just think, we've been gifted the key ingredient to make a delicious pumpkin pie."

I couldn't help but smile at her sunny nature, but as I ran my gaze over Luna, I could see fear and stress hovering beneath the surface. Whatever was in her apartment terrified her. And she must have been desperate to come knocking on my door.

I left the trolls to their lazy lounging, and we headed back inside.

Nugget was perched on top of the pumpkin, while Russell pecked at one side.

"Oh! Don't spoil it. I'm upcycling this gift." Luna hurried over and rolled the pumpkin so the creative etching on the side couldn't be seen. "I'll make us a pie with this. You'd all like that, wouldn't you?" She smiled at Russell and Nugget.

Russell squawked loudly and flapped away. Nugget hopped off the pumpkin and returned to his moldy bedding without saying anything.

I remained in the doorway, watching Luna. Having her here brought back too many memories. I'd slammed the door on my troubled past, and I couldn't pry it open, no matter who asked. And it wasn't my place to help. She should find someone better able to deal with the evil spirit in her home.

Luna looked up at me after she'd finished inspecting the pumpkin, and her gaze lowered. "You're not going to help me, are you?"

"I can't help. I'm no use to you. I probably wouldn't be able to detect the ghost, let alone do anything about it."

"You won't know until you take a look. Half an hour. Just see if you sense anything dark or if you know what he wants. Once I figure out what the ghost needs, I can send him on his way."

I flexed my hands. "I don't have time to help you. And my magic is broken."

"It's not! I can feel—"

"No! The Magic Council made sure I can't cast anything stronger than a weak light spell. Even if I could figure out what your unwelcome ghost wants, I couldn't do anything about it. You need to find someone else."

"I could loan you some of my magic, or we could combine magic. We used to do that when we were younger, and we were scarily powerful when we combined strengths."

"I'm really sorry, Luna, but I need to get on. I've got my own problems to deal with, and I've only got a few days to sort through this whole house. And as you can see by the hulking trolls outside, I've got the Magic Council watching me. One wrong move, and I'll be back inside."

Luna stood and brushed down her knees. "I don't know where else to turn. I... I guess I'll figure something out."

"You should move. That'll get rid of your ghost."

She bit her lip. "And leave him with the next person to tackle. I don't know. Maybe I should. I just love it there. It was heaven until the ghost appeared."

55

Gah! I hated turning her away, but there was no other option.

I grabbed the pumpkin. "Take this with you. You can make that pie. I bet it'll be delicious."

Luna shook her head as she headed to the door. "The pumpkin is probably rotten. See you around, Indigo." She walked out of the living room, and the front door shut softly as she left.

I blew out a breath, trying to sort my churning emotions into order. I didn't care Luna needed help. We'd been out of each other's lives for a long time, and I didn't owe her anything. So why was I feeling so bad? If I didn't care about Luna and her ghost problem, I'd have shut the door in her face the second she'd shown up.

I looked around the room, frustration fizzling through me. I glared at Nugget. "You lot also need to get out of here. I've got work to do. And why did you let me fall asleep?"

"We aren't your personal alarm service," Nugget said.

"You need to leave."

"Someone rolled off the wrong side of the armchair. Why can't we stay where we are while you work?" Nugget said.

"Because you'll get in the way. Out. Now." I pointed at the door. I wanted to be on my own, and I didn't need more reminders of my past bothering me.

Russell, Nugget, and Hilda simply stared at me.

I grabbed a dishcloth and flapped it at Russell. He squawked at me and headed to the door. I pulled

56

it open and waved the cloth until he shot out. "You too, Nugget."

Nugget turned in a circle and settled on the moldy towels.

"Don't make me grab a broomstick and chase you," I said. "Out."

Nugget hissed at me, before jumping off the towels and strutting to the door. "You're not as nice as I remember. Being away from Witch Haven hasn't done you any good."

"Being here didn't do me any good either." I gripped the edge of the door, my knees shaky. It was a mistake to come back here. It was overwhelming. I should have given up everything, all the memories and Magda's magical artefacts, and let the Magic Council do whatever they liked with it.

I turned from the door. "You too, Hilda. I saw you hide behind that jar on the mantelpiece."

She scuttled out, across the ceiling, and out the door.

I stalked back to the kitchen, grabbed food for them, and slung it outside, before slamming the door shut.

I let out a sigh and rolled my shoulders. No more distractions. I had to stay focused on my mission. Fix up this place, then get out of Witch Haven as quickly as I could.

⁂

It was heading toward dusk as I stood with my hands on my hips surveying my progress. I was certain I'd discovered at least two new species of venomous spiders while sorting through the junk left behind by Magda. Fortunately, none of them had bitten me, but I was still covered in dust, my throat was dry, and I had cobwebs stuck to my hair. And I'd only cleared two rooms. This job was bigger than I'd expected.

There was a huge pile to my right that I considered trash, a pile in the middle was for recycling or sending to the goodwill, and another pile that would most likely be burned on a huge bonfire.

My stepmom had been a hoarder. That meant she had several copies of the same spell book, spare wands, and numerous broomsticks that kept appearing as if out of nowhere. She also had an enormous closet of clothes that I hadn't even dared look at.

It was tempting to burn the lot and be done with it, but I couldn't be that callous. I had a fragment of heart left, no matter what the residents of this place thought.

I ran a hand through my hair, grimacing as my fingers stuck in the cobwebs. My stomach grumbled, reminding me I'd barely had anything to eat all day.

I'd have a couple of hours off, clean up, grab something to eat, and then keep on working.

There was no point trying to keep a low profile anymore, not with two hulking great trolls outside, the Magic Council shouting that I was home, and my best friend turning up on the doorstep. So, I'd use the extra time, and just grab a few hours of sleep here and there until everything was sorted and I could leave.

I was hunting through the tins in the kitchen cupboard, looking for something inoffensive to eat, when there was a shriek outside. It sounded like someone had stepped on Nugget's tail.

I hurried to the front door and pulled it open. Luna's uncle, Albert Black, stood by the gate. His wild gaze shifted to me, and he jabbed a finger in my direction. "I should have known there'd be trouble. The second I heard you were back in the village, I got a bad feeling in the pit of my stomach."

"Thanks for the welcome home," I said. "I'm not here to cause trouble. I've come to sort out my stepmom's house." I walked down the porch steps.

Albert was shaking, his face sweaty, and his shoulders tight. "You should never have come back."

"Believe me, I debated that with myself for a long time. I'll stay out of your way. I won't even come into the village." The guy looked a wreck, much older than his sixty something years. I guess that's what grief did to you.

"It's too late for that. You've sealed Luna's fate."

I tilted my head. "Sealed her fate? I've no idea what you're talking about."

"She was here, wasn't she? I told her not to come, but she said you'd help and always looked out for each other."

My stomach dipped as I stepped closer. "Yes, Luna was here, but I sent her away. I can't help with her problem."

59

"That's what I'm talking about. You sent her away. By doing that, you as good as killed her."

Chapter 6

The world felt like it tilted beneath my feet as I stared at Albert. "Luna's dead?"

He barged past the trolls, who looked on with interest, but made no move to intervene. "What did you say to her when she came here?"

"I've already told you, I said I couldn't help her. What's happened to Luna?"

"She was trying to be like you. Luna looked up to you when you were younger and wished she had your abilities so she could be like an Ash witch. I always told her she had enough magic and to be grateful. Luna didn't need to compete to be like you, but she never listened to me."

"You still haven't answered my question. What's happened?" I grabbed his shoulders and shook him.

Fear flashed into Albert's eyes. "She confronted the ghost, just like she asked you to do. She tried to drive it out of the apartment, and it attacked her. You should be the one who's been hurt. She came to you for help and you rejected her."

I swallowed against the lump in my throat. "How badly is she hurt? She's not..." My eyes blurred with tears. My best friend couldn't be dead.

"Luna's alive, but barely. This is your fault. You need to fix this. She'd never have gone up against that ghost on her own if you'd said you'd help."

I pressed my palm against my forehead, massaging the growing ache. "Where is she?"

"At the hospital. The doctor's not sure what to do. The ghost has drained her powers. She's just a shell. My beautiful Luna is dying." A sob shot out of his mouth. "I'll lose her because of you."

"Hey! That's enough blaming me. I made it clear to Luna I couldn't help." The words sounded hollow to my ears. Guilt sliced through me. My best friend could die because I'd turned my back on her.

Albert turned away. "Because you don't care about her. You're still rotten to the core, just like Magda."

"If you think I'm so rotten, why are you here pointing the finger? You should be afraid I'll take you down next." I narrowed my eyes and stepped closer.

Albert trembled some more, but he didn't back away. "You have to help. The ghost has drained Luna almost completely, and the only way to get her back is to destroy it, then her abilities will return. She's being held prisoner by that thing, and it's all because of you."

"First off, it's not. I don't control this ghost. And second, I can't destroy it. I'm not strong enough."

"You can. I witnessed your power for myself when you took my wife away."

I opened my mouth to protest, but I had nothing. "I'm sorry. For everything. But I don't have that power anymore. It was taken from me. Why can't you banish this ghost?"

"My powers don't lie in destruction and death. I bring light and happiness into people's lives by filling their world with magic and cupcakes. Nothing I could do would touch this creature. A twisted beast like that only responds to darkness. The kind of darkness that lives inside you."

"I'm not that bad," I muttered.

"Yes, you are."

I squeezed my eyes shut for a second. I may not have shot out the killing spell that killed Luna's aunt, but I was guilty as charged of being an accomplice.

"What about going to the Magic Council? They're more powerful than me and have better resources. They'll deal with this ghost," I said.

"I suspect you know the way the Magic Council operates much better than I do, but we both know they'd debate their actions for weeks before doing anything. Luna doesn't have that long." Albert sucked in a shaky breath and dabbed at his top lip. "The ghost has attached itself to her and is continuing to drain her. She'll be dead in a few days if you don't do something. It has to be you. Or are you willing to let another innocent die by your hand?"

"I... I can't. You don't understand. I'm not—"

"You're not interested in helping your friend?"

I huffed out a breath. "It's not that."

"Even after everything you and Magda did to this village, Luna still cares for you. She still thinks there's goodness in you. And it just about broke her heart that you never replied when she reached out."

"That was a misunderstanding. I didn't know she'd written to me. I never got her letters."

"So you say," he said. "But now this. She turns to you when she needs you the most, and you shove her away."

"I didn't shove her anywhere. This isn't my problem to repair." I gestured behind me at the house. "I've already got enough going on."

Albert puffed out his cheeks. "Luna didn't say anything after seeing you, but she'd been crying. And she ate three of my maple cream pies when she got back. She always eats those when she's upset."

A small smile crossed my face. I remembered those delicious pies. We used to sneak one out of the huge refrigerator in the bakery and eat it in her bedroom.

"Then she told me she was going back to her apartment," Albert said. "I had no idea she'd tackle that ghost on her own. I'd have gone with her if I'd known. She only did it because you let her down."

"I'd have helped if I could. I don't want Luna getting hurt. But she didn't mention she was going after the ghost if I didn't step in." I lifted my hands. "Besides, my magic doesn't work that way, anymore."

"I suppose you're only interested in the really dark spells. Helping other magic users in distress isn't of interest to you."

I gritted my teeth and squeezed my hands together. No matter what I said, Albert wouldn't believe me. I could tell him I had no magic ability left and the Magic Council had drained me of everything, but he wouldn't get it. My heart went out to him, but there was nothing I could do.

"You need to go," I said. "I can't be involved with this. I'm sorry about Luna, and I wish it hadn't ended this way for her."

His top lip curled. "I should have known I was wasting my time by coming here, but I was desperate. I wanted to believe what Luna said about you, that there was still some goodness inside you and that you made a mistake all those years ago. She was wrong. There's nothing good about you."

I turned away, angry tears shining in my eyes. "You're right. There's nothing good about me. So you'd better leave before bad things happen to you, too."

"You're an evil witch," he muttered. "I'll never forgive you if Luna dies."

I didn't turn around until his footsteps had faded. The two trolls looked at me.

I glared right back at them. "Is there something you want to say?"

They both grunted and turned their backs to me.

I stamped into the house and shut the door, before leaning against it. There was no point in getting involved, I'd only make things worse. I didn't have the power needed to make this right. I should stick with the label I'd been given. I was a bad witch.

I stopped in the doorway of the living room. Nugget, Russell, and Hilda sat in a line in front of me. "I thought I told you lot to get out?"

"You're making terrible decisions," Nugget said. "So we decided to ignore the one about leaving

65

us outside. Besides, it's getting cold. What do you expect us to do, sleep outside all night?"

"It's what you've been doing ever since Magda was arrested. You must be used to it by now." I strode into the room and sank into a chair.

I wasn't being difficult, but I really couldn't help Luna. If I had the ability, I'd drop everything and go after that ghost. But I'd only let Luna and her uncle down if I tried with what was left of my magic.

Hilda scuttled up my leg and came to rest on my shoulder. She pressed a leg against my cheek. "You feel bad."

"I feel terrible. I'm the worst best friend in the world. Although Albert had no right to come here and guilt trip me."

"He's a man in a lot of pain. He only has Luna left."

"Yeah, there's no need to remind me about that. His wife was killed thanks to me."

"He's hurting and lashing out because he's desperate to make sure Luna recovers," Hilda said.

Russell flapped over to the chair and settled on the back. He tapped the top of my head with his beak.

"You're trying to tell me something?" I said.

"He's saying he wants to help Luna," Hilda said. "We all do. She's a sweet witch."

"Then you go fight the ghost," I said. "Maybe Russell can catch it in his huge claws and fly away with it."

I got a sharp tap on the head for that comment.

"You could at least try to help," Hilda said. "Visit Luna and see how she is."

"That's just sending myself on an even bigger guilt trip, and I've had enough of those for one day. She won't want to see me. Luna's in this mess because of me. Well, partly. But she shouldn't have chased after that ghost on her own."

"Enough of the sob story," Nugget said.

I huffed out a breath. "It's true."

"So what if it is? It's no surprise you have an awful reputation around these parts," Nugget said. "And you are to blame. You turned Luna away when she came asking for help."

"Because I didn't think she'd do anything as dumb as this." I thumped my head back, making Russell fly off and dust plume around me.

I wasn't here to save my friend. Why did this have to be so complicated?

Hilda tapped my cheek again. "You could go and take a look at Luna's apartment. You might notice something odd."

"All I'll notice is that I'm a magic using loser who struggles to cast a basic spell these days."

"You are a total loser," Nugget said.

"Thanks for that. Why don't you go outside and find a nice cold pile of mud to sleep on?"

"I'm only agreeing with you. But if you did want help..." Nugget flicked his tail.

"Yes? What's your brilliant idea?"

He licked one paw, taking his time. "Well, you have everything you need right here to amp up your magic again."

I sat forward. "Amp up my magic? And risk the attention of the Magic Council?"

"You've already got their attention," Hilda said.

"And I don't need any more official types strutting around and giving me grief."

"You won't get it. So long as you don't let them find out what you're doing." She did a tap dance on my shoulder.

"What have you got to lose?" Nugget said. "Or are you going to prove to everyone they were right about you all along?"

Chapter 7

After barely any sleep, it was time to get to work. I'd mulled over everything I'd discussed with Nugget, Hilda, and Russell last night, and decided that maybe there was something among Magda's things that could fix Luna's ghost problem. And if there wasn't, and I messed up, there was a cold, unwelcoming cell waiting for me courtesy of the Magic Council.

After I'd taken the world's quickest icy shower, dressed in clean clothes, and eaten a tin of peaches, I stood in the middle of the living room. My gaze was fixed on Magda's magic cabinet.

I'd avoided it yesterday, even though it kept calling to me, reminding me of the hours I'd spent picking through the small drawers and shelves, and wondering at the amazing things my stepmom had inside them.

Her hoarding sometimes produced valuable results. She loved to collect gemstones, crystals, and unusual stones she'd pick up when out on one of her long walks.

She'd often infuse her finds with magic. It could be anything from a light spell to something as powerful as a freeze spell. Stones were easy to carry or wear around your neck, so you'd always have an easily available spell if you needed it, without draining your own abilities.

"What are you waiting for?" Nugget said from his towel bundle in the corner. "Get the cabinet open and let's see what we're working with."

"I thought you weren't interested in helping." I walked to the dark teak cabinet and rested my hand on it.

"I didn't say I was. I just want to see you make a mess of this."

"If I do, I'll aim my misfiring magic in your direction." I turned the small silver key in the cabinet lock and pulled open the double doors.

I sucked in a breath as I stared at the contents. Nothing in here had been touched for years, but it looked immaculate. There was no dust on the shelves, everything was lined up with the labels the right way out, and the wood smelled mildly of lemon wax as if someone had recently polished it.

Hilda scuttled up onto the first shelf. She waggled a leg at me.

I held out a finger to make contact so we could talk.

"This is incredible," she said. "I haven't seen inside here for a long time."

A small smile crossed my face. "I used to play my magic store game in here. I'd pretend to be the cashier, and Magda would buy stones and spells from me in exchange for chocolate-covered candy."

"I remember." Nugget yawned. "You made me wear a small hat with a tassel and pretend to be your assistant."

I laughed. "I'd forgotten about that. You used to be a much nicer cat back then."

"And you used to be a better witch."

My smile faded. "Luna loved this cabinet, too. Magda let us play here for hours. I had no idea what half the spells did, but she trusted me with them."

"Magda always put too much faith in you," Nugget said.

"Quit with the insults, or I'll stuff you and put you on the mantelpiece if you don't keep your fuzzy mouth shut. Or maybe I'll use your paws as a spell ingredient."

He hissed at me. "If you use my body parts in your magic, I'll make sure the spells fail and you explode in a cloud of stinky grossness."

I didn't need Nugget jinxing my magic to make that happen.

"Isn't that a ring of control?" Hilda said.

I looked away from Nugget. "You're right. That thing will pack a punch." My hand hovered over the gold ring with a shimmering ruby set in it.

"It does when you know how to use it correctly," Nugget said.

"There's way more magic in this thing than you'd be able to handle," I said.

"Unlike some people in this room, I have excellent control over my abilities," Nugget said.

"Is that so? Try this." I grabbed a bag of herbs and tossed them over his head.

He gave an almighty sneeze and his fur fluffed out like he'd just been given an electric shock. He squeaked as he flipped onto his back.

"Crud! Nugget, I didn't mean to hurt you." I ran over, but stopped as he doubled in size and turned upright, snarling at me like an adorable baby panther.

"Wow!" I laughed as I backed away, not keen on getting near those massive paws. "I didn't know you could do that."

Nugget growled at me. "What did you think that magic would do?" He lifted one paw and examined it.

"I thought it was a spell of sleep. It smelled strongly of valerian. You were supposed to doze off, not get big and fuzzy." I turned to Hilda. "I should use that spell on you. I'd never risk stepping on you if you were bigger."

"I wouldn't like to be big all the time. I don't want to scare people any more than I do. Even though I'm small, I still send people screaming in the opposite direction. It hurts my feelings. What's so scary about being a spider? I eat annoying flies and bugs, and even the occasional skin flake. I keep the place tidy."

I grimaced at the thought of Hilda chewing on my skin flakes. I scratched my arm as I turned my attention back to the magic cabinet. "Hey, isn't this a bloodstone?" I gently eased the black and red stone out from the drawer and placed it in front of me.

Russell squawked loudly and flapped his wings.

"We sense its power," Hilda said. "You'd better not tangle with that until you've got your magic back to full strength. That could blow your head off. It's been well-used."

I rifled through more drawers. There were bundles of multi-colored candles, witch keys, herbs of every description, herbal spell mixes, small dark bottles of infused oils, charcoal tabs, consecrated salt, and dozens of stones and gems. There was everything a witch needed to make her powers even more incredible, providing they were working, and you hadn't been drained by a soul-void member of the Magic Council. And, if I was going for brutal openness, you weren't a bit scared about unleashing your magic on a community you'd devastated once before with your warped spells.

"There's a magical arsenal in here." I stepped back. "I could have fun with all this stuff."

"What are you waiting for?" Nugget said. "I want to see you blow something up."

"Then you'd better hope I don't test my powers on you." I hurried to the kitchen and returned with a portable cauldron which I sat beside the cabinet. I extracted oil, herbs, charcoal, and a dash of salt, and placed everything inside the cauldron.

"Are you sure you know what you're doing?" Nugget said.

"Nope. But casting spells is like riding a bike." At least, I hoped it was.

I stared inside the cauldron. I was aiming for a simple temperature change spell. Give the atoms a jiggle to warm the place up a bit. I needed to test my power and make sure everything was stable before I chased down this ghost and taught it a lesson.

I took a few deep breaths and closed my eyes, holding my hands over the cauldron. When I had my full power, I didn't need to use a ritual to conjure a spell, but whilst my ability was restrained, I needed an extra boost.

"You're making it smoke," Nugget said.

"It's supposed to do that," I muttered. "Give me a minute. I've got this."

"We should evacuate," Nugget said. "Get out while we still can."

"You're welcome to leave any time you like," I said. "And if you don't want to come back, I'm fine with that."

Hilda jabbed my cheek hard with one leg.

"Ouch! What was that for?" I glanced at her and sighed. "Nugget shouldn't be so mean."

"He's not himself," she whispered in my ear.

"I'm very much myself. But I don't like an inexperienced witch messing with Magda's things." Nugget flipped his ears back and forth.

"They're my things now." I closed my eyes again and focused on the cauldron. A flicker of magic pulsed up my arm. It felt unnatural to have such weak magic. The Ash witches were one of the strongest covens in recorded history. They'd been a respected branch of witches until Magda and I smeared the name into murky oblivion.

That was the last thing I needed to think about. Concentrate on the spell. Bring forth the power, just like I'd been taught.

"There are flames!" Nugget said. "Everybody get out!"

"Stop panicking, you're distracting me."

"Maybe you should try something else if you're struggling," Hilda said, a gentle sadness in her voice, suggesting she also doubted me.

"This is a simple spell. I can do it."

There was a high screeching whizz, a flash of light, and the cauldron flipped in the air and exploded, scattering fragments across the room.

I looked down at my clothes and groaned at the sticky residue coating my pants.

I looked around to make sure everyone was okay and had to press my lips together to stop from laughing. Nugget had a large clump of green goo on top of his head.

"I won't forget this," he hissed out. "Make sure you sleep with one eye open from now on."

I bit my bottom lip. "Sorry, Nugget. I guess my magic is still really screwy."

There was a knock at the door, and I glanced up. I wasn't in the mood for visitors. I ignored the knock and knelt to pick up fragments of the cauldron.

There was another knock. This one more persistent and ongoing.

"Aren't you going to get that?" Hilda said.

"It'll be the trolls. They probably heard the explosion."

"They didn't knock the last time they came in," she said.

"Then it's someone from the Magic Council. They already know I'm messing with magic and have come to arrest me. Or it's a resident from the village telling me to get lost."

Nugget peered out the window. "It's not the Magic Council or the trolls."

"Another pumpkin wielding resident?" I said.

"I don't see any pumpkins. Which is a surprise, given who it is."

I placed the pieces of the cauldron in the trash can, before peeking out the window. My eyes widened. "Huh! What are they doing here?"

"Open up!" Odessa Grimsbane's voice came through the door. "We can hear you in there, Indigo. And the house has already told us you are home."

"I didn't know this house talked." I ducked back as my second visitor, Storm Winter, glanced my way. I hadn't heard from either Odessa or Storm since leaving the village. What were they doing showing up now?

"Odessa has cookies," Nugget said. "You need to let her in. I'm starving."

"You don't eat cookies."

"I'll eat anything if I'm hungry enough." He hopped off the window ledge and sashayed out of the room.

I swiped goo off my clothing, then headed to the front door and cracked it open. "Hey. Is there something I can do you for?"

"I told you she wouldn't remember us," Storm said. Her short dark hair spiked up and her pale blue eyes narrowed. "This was a waste of time."

"No! Of course Indigo remembers us. We haven't changed that much." Odessa was short, curvy, and nearly always smiling. She had round cheeks, a cute button nose, and an infectious giggle.

"I remember you, but I'm kind of busy," I said.

"We could come back another time," Odessa said. "Although we brought you welcome home cookies. I made them."

"And guess what flavor they are?" Storm said.

"Um... pumpkin?" Odessa specialized in pumpkin harvesting and scarecrow wrangling.

"And chocolate chip," Odessa said. Her brow furrowed. "You do remember us, don't you? You aren't just being polite? It's been a while since we last met. Although I'd recognize you anywhere."

"Sure, I know you."

"Indigo doesn't do polite," Nugget said from his position on the stairs.

"We'll only stay five minutes, but it's important we speak to you." Odessa waved the plate of cookies at me.

They did look amazing. I opened the door wider and stepped back. It seemed all my old friends wanted to reconnect. Who'd have thought it after everything I'd done?

Odessa walked into the living room and set the cookies down on one of the few surfaces that hadn't been splatted with spell mixture. She placed her hands on her hips and looked around. "I like what you've done with the place. It's very authentic grunge witch."

"Did you blow something up in here?" Storm also looked around, not seeming nearly as impressed by my recent spot of redecoration as Odessa.

"I was messing around with some of my stepmom's old stuff." I gestured at the cabinet. "Thanks for the cookies, but I do need to get on."

"Then we won't waste any more of your time." Odessa walked over and petted Russell. "Hello, handsome birdie. You must be bored, stuck like that."

Russell preened and rubbed his beak against her hand.

"He's not stuck. He's free to leave any time he likes," I said.

Storm looked at me like I was crazy.

"What?" I gestured at Russell. "He came in here when I arrived. I'm not forcing him to stay."

"Your magic really is messed up," she muttered.

I stared at Russell. That made no sense. What was I missing? "What's so important that you needed to see me?" I expected them to tell me to pack my things and leave.

I glanced at the cookies. As tasty as they looked, I shouldn't eat them, just in case there was something in them that had a nasty side effect. I didn't want to end up with ears and a tail.

Odessa unwrapped the cookies, took one, and offered them to me and Storm.

Storm took a cookie, but I shook my head. I had to get Odessa and Storm out of here so I could focus on helping Luna, or simply blowing up cauldrons.

Nugget walked back in the room, looking mildly less goo covered, as if he'd just speed cleaned himself while sitting on the stairs. He was also back to his normal size.

"Oh, how kind of you. You took in all your stepmom's familiars," Odessa said. "Is Hilda here, too?"

Hilda scuttled out from under a chair and waggled her front legs at Odessa.

"I didn't have much choice in taking them in. They barged into the house and haven't left," I said. "It's weird. I barely remember them. I know Nugget, but the others are blurry. A lot is blurry."

Odessa nodded, a sympathetic look on her face. "I expect it is. You've been through a lot. I came looking for them after you and Magda left the village," Odessa said.

"They didn't leave. They got arrested for multiple homicides and the deadly use of dark magic," Storm muttered.

Odessa pursed her lips and shook her head. "I was worried about them, but they'd disappeared. I figured your stepmom had made arrangements for them to be taken somewhere safe."

"Magda didn't have time to make any arrangements for their well-being. They got left behind."

"Ah, yes. I expect she didn't. It was all a surprise what happened that day."

"Yep," I said, not really wanting to delve into that area of my past, but sensing that was where this was headed. "So... why are you here? Is it about what happened, you know, when I..."

"Turned into a psycho witch?" Storm said.

I pressed my lips together and nodded. She'd always been the blunt one in the group, and age had done nothing to soften that aspect of her character.

"No! Nothing like that. That's in the past," Odessa said. "And we're all allowed mistakes."

"That was an epic mistake," Storm said.

"Storm! We talked about this." Odessa pinched Storm's bare arm.

"Fine. What's to say we haven't just dropped by to see an old friend?" Storm didn't try to hide the sarcasm in her tone. She even exaggerated it.

"You could be, but I doubt you're here to rekindle friendships," I said.

"You're not as dumb as you are evil," Storm said. "And I heard you got your brain fried during rehab. Some reckon it was the best thing that could have happened to you."

"Storm! That's enough." Odessa tried to pinch her again, but Storm dodged out the way.

"Some people are wrong." I rubbed the side of my head. I'd lost count of all the spells used on me. Some had left their mark.

"We don't want to talk about what did and didn't happen," Odessa said. "And that won't help the current situation."

"What's the current situation?" I said.

Odessa bit into her cookie and chewed. "Don't you just love pumpkin spice and chocolate?"

"Odessa! Why are you here?"

She swallowed her cookie. "We're here to plead Luna's case."

"People are saying you made her go up against a ghost," Storm said. "It almost killed her."

I groaned. "Then people are wrong, as usual. And that's what happens when you listen to gossip. I thought you were better than that, Storm."

I glared at her, while Odessa bent and petted Nugget, before feeding him a piece of cookie. She brushed crumbs from her fingertips. "We're all a little different since the last time we met. You're prettier than I remember, Indigo, but you're giving out a weird vibe. What's going on with your magic?"

"Nothing you need to worry about."

"She's had it drained," Storm said. "That's what you're picking up on."

"How do you know that?" The snap in my voice sounded unlike me.

Storm tapped the side of her nose. "Because I listen to gossip. Sometimes it's useful."

"Gossip is Storm's business these days," Odessa said.

"How's that work?" I said.

"She's got her own private investigation agency," Odessa said. "I'm so proud of her."

"You poke around other people's business and get paid for it?" I said. "Lucky you."

"It's great." Odessa grinned and patted Storm on the back. "She's like Miss Marple on steroids."

Storm snorted a laugh. "Thanks, Scarecrow girl."

"Yes, that's me! I'm just about to take over my parents' pumpkin farm. Get me! A business owner. I remember Mrs. McGinty at school saying I'd amount to nothing because I liked to talk to animals more than people. She didn't understand that animals are better conversationalists than people. You two being the exception. And they always tell the truth."

I'd forgotten how much Odessa liked to talk. To people and animals. "I'm happy you both have great careers." I gestured to the door.

"Not yet. That's why we're here, to tell you the truth." Odessa picked up another cookie. "You need to help Luna get better."

"I'll tell you the same thing I told her uncle. I didn't suggest Luna confront that ghost. She came to see if I could get rid of it, but I wasn't able to help. As you've both noticed, there is something funky going on with my magic."

Storm picked up a piece of broken cauldron I missed and turned it over. "You don't say?"

"Of course! That makes total sense. You'd have helped if you could," Odessa said. "Luna is your best friend."

"She was. That was a long time ago."

"Some friendships are built on forever. They take their guidance from the rocks and the sky. Eternal and forever. Never dying." Odessa nodded an encouragement at me.

I glanced at the open cabinet and the ruins of the spell I'd attempted. "If I could figure out a way to get my magic functioning, I'd have taken a swing at this ghost."

"I'm sensing a but," Storm said.

"You see. Storm misses nothing," Odessa said.

I arched an eyebrow. "But even if I could, I don't have much time."

"Which is where we come in," Odessa said. "We'll help you."

"We will?" Storm said. "You didn't mention anything about that. I have cases ongoing. Leads to follow."

"Yes, we will. We're getting the gang back together. Our magic works fine, and Indigo's is just rusty," Odessa said.

"It's way more than rusty," I said. "It's gone."

"No! Magic doesn't die until the person does. Even then it lingers for a while. Your stepmom is still drifting through this place. Well, her energy is. Between us, we'll figure this out. Storm can use her sources to find out what people know about the ghost. And I've got my animal connections, and they always want to help people."

"You've got it all worked out. You don't need me."

Odessa lifted one shoulder, and a flush crossed her cheeks. "You always were amazing with the darker side of magic, and this ghost is definitely dark. He could respond to you. I didn't have much success when I made contact."

"You've seen this ghost?"

"No, just felt him. He gives me the serious creeps. I even started turning down Luna's invitations to dinner because every time I visited, I got sick. Anyone who spends too long in her apartment becomes unwell. And Luna's suffering, although I don't think she realizes how bad she's become."

"She looked tense when I saw her, but I figured that was because she was visiting me. I didn't realize things had gotten so difficult."

"Why would you? You weren't around," Storm said. "And you didn't bother to look us up when you came back."

I waved a hand around, gesturing at the mess. "I have all this to deal with. I don't have time for girly chats."

"This isn't a problem. We can help with this as well," Odessa said. "We'll come by after work and clear things out. I liked Magda before she went all dark. It made me sad to see this place abandoned and knowing it was once showered in love. Now you're here, you can get the house back to how it should be."

I was about to tell her that wasn't my plan, but I stopped. I'd only spent a couple of days here, but was already getting sucked in by all the good memories.

"I told you she wouldn't help," Storm said. "Let's get out of here. I have a job waiting for me."

"Indigo will help, won't you?" Odessa said. "And we'll lend a hand here if you need it. You just have to ask. I can supply all the pumpkin pie if you're running low on food." She glanced at the tin of empty peaches I'd left on the side.

"I'm good."

"I'll bring my cleaning kit. I've been meaning to try my new orange infused polish. Oh, and we could hang dried herbs on all the nails, make the place smell good. And what about the yard? You need someone to look at that. I know a guy. He's affordable and friendly."

"Just say yes," Storm said on a sigh. "You know what Odessa gets like. Behind that sweetness is a heart of steel. Resistance is futile."

"I appreciate the offer to help with the house, but I don't think I can do much about the ghost." I looked at all the magical aides in the cabinet.

"You can. The decision's made. We'll help Luna, then fix up this place." Odessa grinned. "Shall we go now and take a little peek at the ghost?"

Storm smirked and looked away.

Odessa ate more cookie, smiling as she waited for my answer.

It looked like they were going nowhere fast, and neither would my mission to get this place cleared out until I got rid of them. "I'll help Luna, so long as you both leave me alone. And I don't want help to clear the house."

"Oh, you will!" Odessa clapped her hands together. "We have to make it a proper home, so you don't ever want to leave. Now that's all settled, shall we go evil spirit zapping?"

Chapter 8

"This is where Luna lives?" I stared at the pristine whitewashed apartment block with double glass fronted doors and neat pots of flowers outside. "I didn't know baking paid so well."

"It doesn't. Her sugar daddy gave it to her," Storm said.

I snorted a laugh. "Yeah, right. Luna has a sugar daddy?"

Odessa chortled and gave me a friendly whack. "No! She's just good friends with Englebert Whistletop. She started doing his grocery shopping once a week when he was sick. They became friends, and he gave her this apartment."

"For free?" I said.

"I told you he was her sugar daddy," Storm said.

"No! Stop teasing. Luna's paying rent," Odessa said.

"A peppercorn rent. Practically nothing. She doesn't even pay for her utilities," Storm said.

It sounded like Luna had landed on her feet thanks to this rich old guy.

"They came to an arrangement that suits both of them," Odessa said.

"Sure. So long as Luna doesn't mind being shown off on Englebert's arm as his cute little witch," Storm said.

"Stop! It's not like that. But even if it was, would it be so bad?" Odessa said. "Englebert is a respected figure around here."

"Who's old enough and wrinkly enough to be Luna's grandfather," Storm said.

"Englebert owns the boutique hotel chain Silver Sparkles, doesn't he?" I said.

"Yep. Magical luxury wherever you stay," Storm said. "He's rolling in cash. And he has no kids, so he's splurging on his other interest. Younger women."

"Luna would never use a guy for money. And it can't be love. She was never into older guys," I said. "Doesn't she like beefed up football player types?"

"She does," Storm said. "But they don't always come with loads of money and free apartments."

I studied the outside of the building. "So, what's the plan with this ghost? Go inside and tackle him head-on and tell him to get lost?"

Storm backed away as she checked her watch. "You do that. I've got to go. There's a client I need to see."

"I thought you were helping," I said. "Don't you want to come inside and see what's messing with Luna?"

"I've already met the ghost. I won't be long. You check things out and report back." She turned and dashed away.

"I guess it's just the two of us," I said to Odessa.

She shook her head and grimaced. "Storm's right. You look first on your own to get an unbiased opinion. I've been in loads of times, so I already know what it feels like in there."

"You want me to go in alone? With a ghost who drained a much more powerful magic user than me?"

Odessa nodded and smiled. "It shouldn't bother you. And Luna's magic has been strange recently, so her ability isn't consistent. Some days, she has too much, and it's oozing out of her pores, then another day, she's kitten weak. I've never met a magic user with such variable vibrations in their magical energy."

"Could this ghost have been affecting Luna longer than anyone realized? He's making her magic unstable."

"It could be this ghost. Although she's been like it since she came into her full powers. Luna was a late bloomer and showed limited ability until she was eighteen. It was weird how her magic didn't want to show itself."

"Luna had magic when I knew her. Although I missed her magic coming out party."

"Oh, yes! Because of the whole killing spree," Odessa mimed stabbing the air.

"Yeah, you got it. Are you sure you don't want to come in with me?"

"I'm certain. There's an interesting bug over there I want to see. He's new to the village and I have to make sure he's not lost. I'll go check him out, then grab us some coffees. I'll wait out here until you're ready to report your findings." Odessa flitted away to a tree and stared intently at the bark.

She was weirder than I remembered, although she'd always loved having conversations with bugs, birds, or anything furry.

I shrugged. So much for Odessa and Storm's help with this ghost. The second they got close to the building, they turned tail and practically ran off. Not that it mattered. I worked better on my own. I was simply humoring them until I could shake them loose and get back to sorting out my own house problem.

I stepped through the large front doors that took me into the tidy communal hall for the six apartments in the block. There was a wide, well-maintained staircase leading up to where Luna's apartment was located. There was a faint smell of lavender polish in the air. Luna's sugar daddy was definitely looking after her.

I shook my head. She didn't have a sugar daddy. She was just nice to everyone, so deserved to be treated well. Although if I got the chance, I'd have a chat with Englebert, to make sure he wasn't putting pressure on Luna to do anything she felt uncomfortable about.

I reached the landing and walked toward door number six. My eyes narrowed as I got within a couple of feet of it. There was smoke drifting out from under the bottom of the door. Was her place on fire?

I ran the rest of the way and tried the handle. The door opened with ease. I stood on the threshold, gazing at the mass of smoke swirling around the hallway.

"Welcome," a male voice hissed. "Enter at your peril."

I snorted a laugh. "Oh! That's very haunted house. Have you got a spooky script to run through? Will I meet my doom next?"

The smoke intensified and swirled toward me.

I waved it away. "Are you the jerk who's been bothering my friend?"

"You have no friends."

"Point well made. But I had friends, and you've been messing with one of them. I don't like that."

"Come inside and show me how unhappy you are?" The voice reverberated with laughter as if the malevolent spirit in the smoke knew how feeble I was when it came to using magic.

But I wasn't backing down. I was here, and it would be a waste of time to turn back. Besides, what was the worst that could happen? If I did meet my doom, there was no one around to miss me. The Magic Council could sell Magda's house and everything in it. Nugget, Russell, and Hilda could find a new place to settle, and I'd be nothing but a bad memory to anyone who bothered to think of me.

I stepped over the threshold and walked into the hallway. The temperature dropped about fifteen degrees, and I rubbed my hands against my arms.

"You should have a warning notice up about the conditions in here. I'd have brought a sweater."

"I can make it hot if you prefer. I hear Ash witches like to burn in hell these days."

"I'm impressed you know who I am. Why don't you introduce yourself?"

"I'm your worst nightmare."

I chuckled. "Yep, you're reading your terrifying lines of horror from a tired old script. You need better scares."

A growl filled the air.

"Down, Fido. Let's get this over with. Get your ghostly claws out of Luna and leave her alone. And pack your smoky bags and get out of here whilst you're at it. You're not welcome."

"Neither are you. This whole village hates you."

"That's not a surprise to hear. I know what I did. Although I'm interested in learning how you recognize me."

"You'd be better off dead."

I pressed my hand over my mouth and faked a sob. "Really? I'm wounded. Listen, jerk, I got that figured out a while ago. Don't worry, I don't expect to live for much longer. I'm here because of a guilt trip and because I have a lot of people to say sorry to. If this is one way I can make it up to Luna, then that's what I'm doing."

"You won't live for long now you're here." The door behind me slammed, and a gust of cold wind that had a faint stench of decay rushed past me, blowing my hair back.

I headed along the hallway and entered the living room. It was just as cold and menacing in here, and goosebumps prickled all over my skin. There was a large, black damp patch on one wall.

91

"I doubt Luna thinks much of your redecorating skills. You should take that paint back and get a refund. Mildew chic will never catch on."

"Luna's not here, anymore. I'm playing with her now."

"It's time you left." This had just gotten deeply creepy. I slid my hand into my jacket pocket and clutched the tiger opal I'd selected from Magda's magic cabinet. The magic fizzled strongly against my fingertips.

I had a plan. It wasn't a great one, but then I'd never dealt with an evil ghost sucking the life out of a friend before, so I was willing to give anything a go.

"Show yourself to me," I said. "It's not fair you get to hide in the smoke while you can see me. Anyone would think you're afraid."

"Your hair would turn white if you knew who I was."

"If it did, I could always dye it if that color didn't suit my skin tone."

A growling laugh echoed around me. "Smart mouthed witch."

"Not so smart, but I don't have many figs to give about what's dumb and what's clever. You can do what you like with me, and—"

The ghost punched through me, sending shards of ice cascading through my veins, erupting into a splitting headache behind my eyes, and then racing down to my toes to freeze them to the point of pain.

I staggered back, my breath pluming out of me. "Hey! That's just rude."

92

The ghost swirled around me in the smoke. "You're a broken Ash witch. This will be interesting."

I waved my arms in the air and jogged on the spot, trying to get the feeling back into my extremities. I'd never been punched by a ghost before. It was zero fun.

"Reveal yourself, spirit. Tell me why you're here. There must be a reason you've chosen to focus on Luna. Has she done something to make you unhappy?"

"It's nothing personal. Not with her, anyway. Although she has too many secrets. It's time they came out."

"I don't care if she has a thousand secrets. Stay away from my friend and leave her home." I tightened my grip on the tiger opal, and heat washed up my arm. The sensation reminded me of the flares of magic I got when learning how to control my power. It felt good to have a taste of that magic again. I'd missed it.

The ghost continued to swirl around me, laughing and growling. Despite the cold, sweat broke out on my brow. The energy exuding from this ghost was pure darkness. I'd only sensed that once before, and that was when Magda finally lost control.

I focused on the ghost's movement. It was shifting in a figure-of-eight pattern, circling me in big, lazy waves.

I needed to time this right. I'd only get one shot with this tiger opal. This was a one trick spell. I positioned myself in the center of the room so nothing would get in my way.

As it grew colder and my teeth chattered, I thrust out my hand and opened it to reveal the tiger opal just as the ghost shot straight through it.

A roar filled the room. It was so loud I slapped one hand over my ear.

The light vanished from the room.

I held my breath, waiting to see what the ghost would do next. The temperature was returning to normal as a dark red glow began in one corner.

I hurried over and pulled out the small wooden box I'd brought with me. It was an ancient containment box Magda had stored in her cabinet. Despite it not being used for years, it held strong magic. I should be able to contain this ghost for a short time until I got it out of the apartment.

That was as far as my plan went. Get the ghost out of here and make it release Luna from his hold. After that, who knew?

I swept the box over the dull red smear. Had I damaged the ghost with the tiger opal? It had certainly stopped its mocking, and the smoke had almost vanished.

But if this was what was left of the ghost, no matter what I did, I couldn't capture the smoky red color. And I needed to contain it, because it was expanding.

"Tell me who you are. Show me why you're here and then leave. Spirit, leave this place and don't come back." I pulled out a bottle of salt spray and blasted it at the red smear. If I'd weakened the ghost, a banishment incantation could work. I could drive him out of this apartment and he would be homeless. Just like anybody, ghosts hated to have no home of their own. They'd drift around aimlessly with no anchor. It was easy to get blown off course and find yourself lost if you had nowhere to call home.

I tried the banishment again, continuing to move the containment box through the red smear, while squirting out the salt spray. Nothing took. If this was what was left of the ghost, then he didn't want to go anywhere.

The back of my T-shirt was yanked, and I yelped as I was lifted off my feet and flung against the wall.

A large inky mass with glowing yellow eyes loomed over me, and smoky swirls that looked like claws raked through the air in front of my face. "You'll never trap me, witch. I'm too powerful for you."

"You're only this powerful because you've been feeding off Luna and her fear. Once she's free from your grip, you won't be so cocky. I'll get you then." I flinched as the smoky claws raked across my skin, leaving behind an icy ache.

"Maybe you will, but I'm too strong for you now. And when you're dead, you won't be able to do a thing to stop me."

I was flipped off my feet, the window flung open, and I was tossed outside.

My panicked brain had five seconds to process that I was about to hit bone crunchingly hard concrete. I plundered my terrified thoughts, trying to find a spell to save me. All I got was a blank wall of terror. I was in trouble.

When I'd said I didn't have long to live, I didn't realize the end was so near.

K.E. O'CONNOR

I was bracing for impact, when a dark-clad figure rushed forward and caught me in his arms.

Chapter 9

My speed and weight meant that even though my mystery savior caught me, we still slammed into the concrete hard enough to cause bruises and crunch bone.

A pained grunt came from beneath me as I lay stunned from my fall from the window.

I rolled off the guy who'd saved me and held out my hand. "Thanks for the catch. I wasn't... oh, it's you."

Olympus Duke lay at my feet, his eyes unfocused. His gaze snapped to me and he frowned. "I see you're finding trouble to get into, even though you've only been back here a short time." He moved smoothly to his feet and brushed down his dark jacket.

"I was trying to help a friend." I lowered my hand as my shoulders slumped. My visit had been an epic failure.

His gaze shifted to the apartment. "Who lives here?"

"Luna Brimstone."

"I've heard that name in the village. Is that the witch who was attacked by a ghost?"

"Yes. She asked me to help her with her ghost problem."

"Then you've wasted your time and risked your life. You're aware of your limited magic situation. So unless you're breaking the terms of your probation, there's nothing you can do here. You haven't been using magic items you shouldn't, have you?"

I'd dropped the tiger opal and the box as I'd been flung out the window, so there was no evidence of my guilt. "Magic takes all kinds of interesting forms."

"Is that a yes?"

I gave him my sweetest smile. "I'm always innocent."

Olympus grunted. "Why get involved with something you have no control over?" His sharp gaze traveled over me.

"Because I felt guilty. And I keep telling people I'm no good to them, but they don't listen. So, I came to take a look. That's when the ghost threw me out the window."

Olympus' gaze flicked to the smashed window. "You could have been killed."

"I'd have only broken a few bones. It wasn't that big a drop. But it's a good job I had such a soft landing."

He grunted again and flexed his arm muscles.

I hid a grin. "You hate me. Why did you bother catching me?"

"I didn't know it was you. I saw someone come out the window and acted on instinct."

"You're a real superhero."

The corner of his mouth tilted up. "We're not all so bad at the Magic Council."

"You are in my experience, but thanks for the save." Even though I was certain Olympus wouldn't have helped if he'd known it was me. If I was dead, that was a big problem gone for the Magic Council.

"I'm glad I caught you," he said.

"Quite literally."

This time, a smile lit his face, making him look much less severe. "Indeed. But you misunderstand me. You need to come with me."

"Um... no. I don't need to go anywhere with you." I crossed my arms over my chest.

"You have no choice. The Magic Council will require an explanation for what's gone on here. If you're interacting with dangerous spirits—"

"I'm not! Not deliberately. I didn't go to Luna's apartment to find a badly behaving friend to mess around with. I was doing her a favor."

"You know the rules of your rehabilitation. No involvement with dark magic. That involves casting spells, administering curses or hexes, or associating with those who dabble in the dark arts."

"I had no clue this ghost was a dark arts dabbler. And he may not be. It may be that he's a huge jerk who's messing with my friend to amuse himself. I didn't visit the apartment to find trouble."

"You should have known you'd get in trouble. It follows you everywhere. Come with me. This won't take more than a few hours."

"I'm going nowhere with you." I stepped back as Olympus reached for me.

"Limpy! I didn't know you were still in Witch Haven." Odessa hurried over, a smile on her face.

He slid a glance her way, his cheeks flushing red. "I wish you wouldn't call me that."

Odessa chuckled. "It's cute. Olympus makes you sound so scary. Limpy is much nicer."

I snorted a laugh, which earned me a scathing glance from Limpy.

"How did you get on in Luna's apartment?" Odessa passed me a large takeout mug of coffee.

I pointed at the broken window. "Not so great. He's not Casper the friendly spook."

Her eyes widened. "You came out that way?"

"Yep. And Limpy caught me. He saved me from a few broken bones."

"Don't call me that," he grumbled.

"I could shorten your name to Pus. How's that work for you?" I said.

Olympus growled. "I don't need my name shortened to anything."

"Why didn't you use a spell to soften the impact of your fall?" Odessa said.

I pointed a thumb at Olympus. "He can tell you the answer to that question."

He narrowed his eyes at me. "It's in the best interest of the village that Indigo has no opportunity to cause trouble while she's here."

Odessa wrapped an arm around my shoulders. "She's here to help us. You shouldn't stop her from using magic to keep herself safe."

"It's more a case of keeping others safe," he muttered.

Odessa shook her head. "You are a grumpy bear. I'm glad Indigo's opening up her stepmom's house and bringing it back to life. It'll be good to see the place occupied again. It made me so sad to see it empty."

"That's not... I haven't decided what I'm doing with the house. Don't get your hopes up about me coming in and doing a makeover." Although I had no plans to stay, I didn't want Olympus blabbing about what was going on any more than he already had. He was dying to get his hands on Magda's property, and couldn't wait to see me out of the village.

"We'll have a big welcome home party when you're ready," Odessa said. "I'll bring my special pumpkin spiced muffins. I'll even get some of the friendlier scarecrows to do a dance. Some of them have been practicing for months. They're almost coordinated."

"No parties," Olympus said. "The new owners may not want that."

"New owners?" Odessa's expression fell. "That house has to stay in the Ash witch family. Ash witches have lived there for hundreds of years. The house won't like it if it changes hands."

"The house won't get a say," Olympus said.

"It will! It knows something is going on," Odessa said. "I need to see how it's feeling. It could be unsettled with all this change."

"We'll talk about this later," I said. "Haven't you got somewhere you need to be, Olympus?"

He arched an eyebrow. "You should come with me."

"I'm busy. And unless you have a warrant for my arrest—"

"That can be arranged."

"Until you do, I'm staying here."

He pointed at the broken window. "I'll be drawing this matter to the attention of other members of the Magic Council. They won't be happy to hear you're associating with this ghost."

"Oh, Indigo's done nothing wrong," Odessa said. "This is a misunderstanding. Limpy, you must let me know if you or any of the Magic Council members need my special pumpkins this year. I'm already getting orders, and I'd hate for you to miss out."

His gaze remained on me. "Sure. I'll let them know." He glared at me for a few more seconds, before turning and walking away.

"What are you doing, offering the Magic Council special pumpkins? Have you got a bribery system set up so they leave you alone?"

Odessa winced. "Bribery is such a bad word. My pumpkins keep them happy, and that seems to keep them out of my way. I find a little gentle enticement works wonders on them."

I shook my head. If only that was the solution to my problem with the Magic Council. I had a bad feeling Olympus wouldn't leave Witch Haven until I did, and I hated him watching me.

"So, no luck with the ghost?" Odessa said.

"No. I thought I had him for a moment, but he was playing with me. I used one of my stepmom's tiger opals to weaken him. It seemed to work, but I couldn't capture what was left of the ghost. Then he doubled in strength and tossed me out the window. It's weird though. His power felt familiar, and he knew me." I stared up at the broken window. "It felt like I'd faced that magic before, but I can't remember where."

"I'm sure you have. Magic moves in circles. It comes around on itself and you bump into your past."

"Um, I guess so."

"Did you use a ghost trap?"

"I used one of Magda's containment boxes. It had enough energy to contain the essence of a ghost, but it didn't work."

"I've got several. They're amazing. You can use one of mine if you like the next time. The power is fresher."

"There's going to be a next time? I said I'd take a look. I have and can't see how to catch this ghost."

"That was just a first try. Now you know what you're dealing with, it'll be simple."

"Says the woman who didn't come in to help."

Odessa glanced over her shoulder at the tree. "I was right about that bug. He was lost. So I was helping, just not you."

I shook my head. "What do you use ghost traps for?"

"Trapping scarecrows."

"You've lost me."

"Some of them can be mean. They get possessed with the wrong energy, and even something stuffed with straw and a pumpkin for a head can be dangerous. And as autumn creeps closer, they get more powerful. I'm thinking I need to hire an assistant."

"An assistant scarecrow wrangler. That would be an interesting job description to put together."

"It would be a fun job for anyone brave enough to take it on. I'll give it some thought. It takes a special someone to deal with the scarecrows." She caught hold of my arm. "How about we go get something to eat?"

"I could eat."

"We'll go to Fandango's. We can tell Albert the good news." Odessa tugged me along the sidewalk.

"There's good news in all this mess?"

"There is. You're going to get Luna better."

"I make no guarantees. And my first attempt at dealing with that ghost was a failure."

"It was a learning experience. You've got an idea of what you're dealing with now, so when you go back with my ghost traps, you can catch him easily."

"Nothing about this job will be easy. That ghost was full of hate. He called Luna a plaything."

"He's mean. Almost as mean as some of my scarecrows."

We walked along in silence for a moment as we headed toward the center of the village.

My stomach tightened, and I lowered my head. I hadn't meant to come into the village. I'd planned to stay at Magda's house, get it emptied, and then leave. Instead, I'd gotten myself tangled in a ghost mystery that had nothing to do with me.

I glanced around at the people walking by, but they didn't pay me any attention. Maybe we could sneak in, grab some food, and get out again before I drew any trouble to me.

I glanced around, taking in my old stomping ground. There were several new stores I hadn't noticed when I'd first arrived. There was a pet store, a bookstore, and an expensive-looking dress store.

I hurried us along, keen to keep away from any curious gazes. The second people recognized me, there'd be problems.

We headed into the bakery, and I closed my eyes for a second and inhaled the memories of the hours I'd spent eating cherry buns, lemon slices, and sugar sponge cakes as I did my homework with Luna.

The place hadn't changed a bit. There was still a huge glass-fronted cabinet containing all the delicious treats. There were half a dozen wooden tables at the back of the small store, and the tempting smell of sugar and warm chocolate filled the air.

"We should get sandwiches and cake," Odessa said. "Ghost hunting is hungry work."

"You haven't been ghost hunting. You disappeared to talk to some bug."

"I'm hungry from watching you work." She grinned. "What will it be?"

"You order for us. I've just spotted Albert at the back. I want to talk to him."

She patted my arm. "Good idea. Put his mind at rest. Everything will soon be sorted."

I wished I had half her confidence. I walked past the tables toward Luna's uncle. He was hunched over, scrubbing a spot on the floor with a mop.

"Albert. I'm glad I bumped into you."

He turned, and his eyes narrowed. "Get out. You're not welcome here."

"I'm not surprised to hear that, but I wanted you to know I'm going to help Luna if I can."

He stared at me, his hands tight around the broom handle. "You are? Don't expect to get paid."

105

"I'm not doing it for the money. I'm doing it because Luna and I were once friends. I only turned her away because I didn't think I could help. I didn't think she'd get hurt. I'm sorry for that."

He let out a sigh, and his shoulders slumped. "I'm sorry, too. I shouldn't have shown up and yelled at you. I panicked when I learned what had happened to Luna. I'm so scared she won't make it through this." His jaw wobbled and tears filled his eyes.

"I've already been to her apartment. I've met the ghost who hurt her. He's powerful, but I'm trying to figure out how to deal with him."

"You can destroy it? You have the dark power to do that?"

I didn't want to burst the tiny bubble of hope that bloomed around Albert. "I still have some power. I'll use it for good."

He cleared his throat several times before patting his chest. "I appreciate that. I didn't mean all those things I said to you."

"You were right to say them. What happened all those years ago was wrong. I regret it. I wish it had never happened."

"We all wish that." His gaze flicked over me. "I really liked Magda. I wish you hadn't both gone bad."

"Same here." I looked away, staring at the chalkboard full of descriptions of delicious cakes. Being back in Witch Haven, I was remembering the good times. Those last few unstable weeks had blotted out all the great memories. I'd loved living here, and I'd never wanted to leave. And there was still that small blank in my memory that refused to budge. Why had we done it? Why had we let loose that dark magic on the village and destroyed so many lives? It was a question I'd been asked, and asked myself, hundreds of times, without coming to a resolution.

"I've got food." Odessa sing-songed as she danced over with a huge brown paper bag in her hands. "You make the best cake, Albert. I've got four different slices to try."

"I'm always happy to hear when my customers are satisfied," he said.

"Let me know when you need some pumpkins for your window display," Odessa said. "And when you're getting low on pumpkin filling. I'm growing a new South American variety. It's extra sweet and would be ideal in a sweet crust pie with coconut cream and chocolate shavings."

"Thanks, Odessa. I'll get an order in soon." Albert's gaze shifted to me, and he gave a small nod.

Odessa grinned at me. "Is everything good?"

I nodded. It wasn't good, but I was feeling a bit better. And if there was the slightest chance I could catch this ghost and help Luna, then I'd take it.

She gave my arm a gentle squeeze and lifted up the bag full of goodies. "Perfect. Then let's go eat."

Chapter 10

"If we position a trap by the front door, the hallway, and then in the room where the ghost attacked me, that should cover most of the areas." I stood outside Luna's apartment door, peering at the light hazy smoke in the hallway with Odessa.

"Whatever you think best," she whispered.

"Are you coming in this time?"

"No! I'll stand here and give useful instructions."

"Anyone would think you're scared of this thing."

"That ghost threw you out a window," Odessa said. "I'm your functioning back up so I can run for help if it happens again."

"Why can't I be the functioning back up?"

"Because... you know, you're so good at the dark stuff. If I throw sparkles at this ghost, it'll probably laugh itself to death. If that's even possible. Can you kill a ghost?"

"We're about to find out." I looked at the ghost traps we'd collected from Odessa's house after eating our treats from the bakery. "You'll have to talk me through how to set these things up." Three innocuous looking brown wicker baskets sat by Odessa's feet. I'd never seen anything that looked less like a ghost trap in my life, but she assured me they worked, and I could feel a faint hum of magic running through them. It had an Odessa-like vibe, warm, slightly fuzzy, and inviting.

"They're super easy to use. Place the basket on the ground where you want it, stroke it five times, and say activate."

"Why does it need stroking?"

"The magic needs coaxing. Kindness is the way to do that."

"Got it. Stroke the magic into life." I stepped over the threshold and into the apartment. The temperature instantly dropped, but I ignored it as I set the basket down. Five swift strokes and nothing happened. I looked over at Odessa, who remained firmly on the outside of the apartment.

"No! Not like that! Show the trap some love. And take your time. Don't do a hit it and quit it move," Odessa said.

"That's one thing we don't have. If this ghost comes for me again, I need these traps ready."

"Then be kind to the basket, and the basket will be kind to you. You reap what you sow. I've learned that by growing pumpkins."

I groaned and tried again, feeling uncomfortable as I gently stroked a basket. This time, it worked. The basket hummed and wobbled on its base, before sparkles of orange drifted from the surface.

"You got it," Odessa said. "You see. You can still control magic."

"It's your magic. And it's pure magic. You're the whitest witch I've ever met."

"Don't be too sure of that. I've had to wrangle a fair few evil scarecrows in my time, and they don't respond well to white magic."

"I can't believe you've ever used anything dark. It's not in you." Some of us were tempted by the darkness and others weren't. Odessa was a hundred percent in the good witch category.

Her smile faded. "It's in all of us when it needs to be. Hurry up and activate the next two traps. We've got a mean ghost to catch."

I set the second basket at the end of the corridor, gave it five loving strokes, and then asked it to activate. It did. No problem at all. And there was no ghost bothering me. This could work.

"We've got this ghost running scared," I said. "He must know he's in trouble."

"He does now you're here," Odessa said. "Did that trap work?"

"It's glowing nicely. Two down, one to go." I looked back at Odessa. The open door seemed a long way away. "Are you sure you don't want to come in and lend a hand? I could do with someone who can cast an awesome spell if things go wrong."

"I'll stand guard here, just in case the ghost tries to get out this way."

I shook my head, took a deep breath, and turned to face the living room. This was where things had gotten bad the last time I'd visited.

It was much colder this far into the apartment, and the end of my nose grew numb as I walked into the room.

There was a small amount of smoke in the air, but the ghost wasn't stirring. Maybe I had weakened him during my last visit. He definitely hated the tiger opal. I should have brought more with me. Maybe I could have defeated him if I'd had enough. But then there was still the problem of trapping what was left.

Odessa's traps would work. We were close to success. I could feel it.

I stopped in the middle of the room and set down the final basket. I stroked it five times and asked it to activate. Nothing happened. I tried again. Still no joy.

I headed back to the corridor. "Odessa, this last basket isn't working."

"Oh! I must have picked up the tricksy one."

"You have a tricksy trap?"

"I have one that likes to be tickled before it activates."

"You're joking?"

"No joke. Tickle its bottom."

"Seriously?"

"The traps are sensitive. They do dangerous work and need a little reward tickle. That'll get it humming."

Her magic was so bizarre. Still, I needed this trap to activate. I headed back into the room, knelt beside the basket and arched an eyebrow. "Don't give me any problems, buddy. Odessa says you like a little scratch and tickle before you get to work."

The basket trembled a fraction.

I tipped it on its side, gave it a little scratch on a rough patch and a pat for good measure. Then I stroked down the sides.

I fell back as a blast of light shot out the top of the basket and it bounced from side to side.

"It looks like you're one happy little basket. Whatever works for you, I guess."

"Did you get it going?" Odessa said.

"Yep. One weird, kinky basket activated," I said.

"Perfect. Now all we need to do is wait."

***

Three hours passed since I'd activated the ghost traps. Odessa was asleep, slumped against the door, snoring softly. The moon was rising in the sky, and I was bored rigid and freezing cold.

I'd positioned myself in the hallway, so I could see all three traps. Nothing had touched any of them.

My head jerked up, and I frowned. I couldn't doze off on the job, not with some malevolent ghost waiting to grab me.

I tilted my head. Something had disturbed me from my unplanned snooze. The trap nearest to Odessa looked untouched, as did the one at the other end of the hallway. I peered at the one in the living room. It was moving.

I edged closer. "Odessa," I whispered. "I think we've got something."

She lifted her head and yawned. "About time."

I reached the living room door and stopped. The trap was bulging and the orange light flowing from the top had turned gray.

"Get in here," I said to her. "I don't know if this has trapped a ghost, or it's just broken."

"Is it safe?"

"Probably not. But you need to see if this trap has activated."

Odessa tiptoed over to me and grabbed my shoulder. She squeaked and bounced on her toes. "It's worked. You got it."

"There's a ghost inside the trap?"

"Yes! The light changes color when something's been caught." She nudged me. "Go get it."

I raced over to the trap and touched the side. I yanked my hand back just as fast. The basket was icy cold. I looked up at Odessa and grinned. "We've got one ghost inside here."

She did a bounce in the air and jigged on her toes. "Well done. Now Luna will get better."

"It's a good first step, but we still need to make sure this ghost let's go of her."

"He's in your control now. Whoever owns the trap, owns the ghost."

"Then technically, this ghost is yours. Do you want him?"

She backed away. "Not a chance. I don't want a ghost rampaging through my pumpkin patches and terrifying my scarecrows."

"Can a scarecrow be scared? Aren't they the essence of scare?"

She waved a hand at me. "You know what I mean. Grab the basket and let's get out of here."

I went to touch the basket again, but then stopped. "What do you normally do with the ghosts once you trap them?"

"Um, well, the things that take control of my scarecrows aren't often mean like this ghost. I give them a stern warning and send them on their way.

They're usually just bored spirits looking for fun and take things too far."

"You don't know what we should do with this ghost?"

"We'll figure something out. The basket will hold him for a while. We can work out what to do with the ghost once we're out of here. Let's move. This place is giving me the chills."

"I can take him to Magda's house. There's plenty of magic there to keep him contained."

"Yes! Great idea. We'll do that, then go see how Luna's doing. Even just trapping the ghost may be enough, and he'll loosen his hold on her."

I grabbed the basket, sucking in a breath at how icy cold it was against my skin. This had to work. We'd got the ghost. Now all we had to do was figure out how to get rid of him. Then Luna would get well, and I could finish my task and get out of Witch Haven.

There was no way I could get attached to this place again. It wasn't my home. It was just a temporary stopping point. A short diversion. I'd soon be back on track. Then I'd be away from the unwelcome scrutiny of the Magic Council, back in my own space, my silence, and my solitude.

"Your days are numbered, ghost," I muttered. "Once I get rid of you, I can get out of here."

Odessa turned as she picked up the other magic baskets. "What was that? Did you say you were leaving?"

"Oh! Well, yes." I lifted one shoulder, trying to ignore the concern in her eyes. "Odessa, there's no place for me here. Apart from you and Luna, everyone hates me."

"That's not true. Well, it sort of is, but only because the rest of the villagers don't know you. They remember the Indigo from the time before. You're different now."

"I'm not so different."

"You must stay. Your place is here. You're an Ash witch."

I shook my head. "Not anymore. I've got a different life. And I've found a place where people don't disturb me and I can be on my own."

She wrinkled her nose. "Isn't that lonely?"

"I'm not lonely."

"What about your friends?"

I adjusted the basket in my arms. "What about them?"

"You have friends, right? You've made friends since you left Witch Haven?"

"You mean when I was dragged away and slung in rehab? There's not much chance to make life long buddies in a place like that."

"Um, yes. There must have been someone you bonded with. You can't have been on your own all this time."

"It's not so bad. Besides, it's not easy making friends as you get older."

Odessa's sad little sigh twisted my heart. "What do you do for fun at the weekends?"

I shrugged off her concerns. "I do just fine. The way I live now means no one else will ever get hurt. It's better this way."

"Not for you. I wouldn't like living on my own," Odessa said. "You should consider staying. I want you to stay."

A tiny part of me did too, but it wasn't happening, and I didn't want to deal with any more of Odessa's sympathy. "Let's deal with this ghost, get the trap out of here and back to Magda's house. Then we can see Luna and tell her the good news."

I pretended not to notice the flicker of concern in Odessa's eyes as we left the apartment. I'd made the right decision. There was no point in changing my mind. I wasn't staying here. I was here to deal with a problem and then move on. End of story.

Chapter 11

Odessa and I must have looked like we were in a speed walking contest as we hurried away from Luna's apartment.

I had the icy basket containing the ghost held out in front of me so I didn't get ice burns. I tugged the sleeves of my sweater down over my hands to take the edge off the cold, but it was still seeping through and numbing my fingers.

"Have you any idea what we should do with this once we get back to the house?" I said to Odessa.

She glanced at me and bit her bottom lip. "I was hoping you'd have an idea. You were always into ghosts when we were younger."

"Not trapping evil ones."

The basket wriggled in my hands as if it were alive, and I tightened my grip. "We have to keep the ghost weak. And we need to find out why he's after Luna and then make sure he lets her go."

"We could try asking nicely," Odessa said. "It's what I do when the spirits take over my scarecrows."

"That always works?"

117

"Most of the time. They see reason and go on their way. Most of them have simply gotten lost as they move on. I help to guide them to the right path."

"From the feel of this ghost, I don't think he's ever been on the right path, even when he was alive. We need to zap his energy, force him to loosen his hold on Luna, and then destroy him."

Odessa was quiet for a moment. "We could rehabilitate him. It worked for you."

"Yeah, look at me. I'm living the dream."

She squeezed my elbow. "You're doing better than you think. You're too hard on yourself."

The ghost trap wriggled again, and I welcomed the distraction. Odessa had no clue about the mess my life was in, and I had no plans to tell her. "Let's hurry. This spirit wants to get loose."

We jogged the rest of the way to Magda's house, which was my least favorite activity to do, but these were desperate times, and raced through the front door.

I dropped the basket on the floor, flexed out my fingers, and then rubbed them to get the feeling back in them.

Nugget uncurled from his pile of bedding in the corner and rolled onto the floor. "What have you brought in here? It smells terrible."

"Hey, Nugget. It's the ghost who's been bothering Luna," Odessa said.

Nugget sniffed the basket, then backed away, his fur bristling.

Russell squawked from his perch, then zoomed out the open window.

118

The basket bulged and tipped from side to side.

"Hmmm. It's never done that before," Odessa said.

"The ghost's trying to get out." I grabbed the basket to keep it steady. "Give it a magic boost."

Odessa rolled up her sleeves and pressed a hand on either side of the basket. She closed her eyes and gritted her teeth.

The basket continued to wriggle, and the room grew colder.

"Keep going," I said. "It's not making any difference."

"I haven't had time to recharge," Odessa said. "I infused these baskets with magic before I brought them over. I'm running on half power."

"Don't give up. We can't let this ghost get out."

Odessa's face paled. "I've got nothing left. You try."

"I won't have any effect." I waggled my fingers. "The Magic Council made sure of that."

Odessa dropped her hold and frowned. "Try! See what you can do."

Smoke drifted out the top of the basket.

I backed away. "He's getting out!"

"Use your magic," Odessa said.

I scowled at the basket. My magic was too weak to make a difference. If this ghost wanted to get free, there was nothing I could do to stop him.

"The magic is breaking down. Hurry!" Odessa gestured at the basket with a shaky hand.

I felt around inside me for flickers of magic that may do the trick, but with the recent drain from Olympus and breaking the house wards, I had nothing.

I stepped back. "It's too strong for me."

"Don't give up," Odessa said. "We can do this. We'll try together. Put your hands over mine."

I shook my head. "You'd better get out the way. The basket is about to open."

I didn't miss the hint of disappointment in Odessa's eyes as she stepped back from the basket. I was only telling the truth.

A groaning came from the basket as more gray smoke drifted out the top.

"It's going to blow," Odessa said. "We should—"

There was a loud bang, the lid flew open, and smoke flooded into the room.

I ducked, covering Nugget and Hilda who stood beside me, just before a wave of gross smelling smoke covered us.

"What have you messed up this time?" Nugget said from beneath me.

"Nothing! I wanted to get rid of Luna's ghost."

The smoke swirling around the room increased in speed, before flitting out the open window.

I looked up to see Odessa standing upright. All her hair stood on end and her eyes were wide.

I raced over to her. "Did the ghost hurt you?"

She blinked rapidly. "No! I just got taken by surprise. My baskets have never done that before."

The front door opened, and I tensed. Please don't be the Magic Council. If they showed up now, there was no way I could conceal this mess. There was still smoke in the air, and a thick gooey residue encased the basket.

Storm appeared in the doorway, a bag in her arms. Her gaze swept around the room before returning to me. "Wow! You really messed up this time."

I grimaced at her. "Thanks for nothing. Maybe we'd have gotten rid of the ghost if you hadn't raced off the second I needed you."

She shrugged. "I got a lead on a job. Bills don't pay themselves. But I brought snacks."

Odessa walked over, smoothing her hands over her wild hair. "Oooh! What did you bring us?"

"Cookies." Storm glanced at Odessa's messy hair. "Exactly what have you two been up to? I thought you were just taking a look at the ghost, not... this." She gestured at the mess.

"This is the result of our unsuccessful ghost wrangling," I said.

We settled on the chairs in the room and all grabbed cookies.

"Indigo caught the ghost," Odessa said. "In one of my traps. We decided to bring him back here, to figure out what to do with him."

"I'm guessing he escaped?" Storm pointed at the goo coated basket.

"We tried to keep him in there, but he got out. He was too strong," I said.

Odessa opened her mouth, glanced at me, then snapped it shut. "That's right. We did everything we could. We used our magic to keep the seal on the trap intact, but it failed."

"So, why don't we summon him back?" Storm said.

"I didn't know you were a ghost summoner," I said.

121

"I'm not. But I can't be any worse than either of you when it comes to dealing with ghosts."

"I haven't seen you deal with any ghosts since I got here," I said. "I was the one left to hunt this thing out alone."

She gave another shrug. "That's because I'm busy making a living. If we combine magic, we could force this thing to talk to us and see what it wants, then figure out a way to get rid of it." Storm took a large bite of chocolate chip cookie.

"I'm in," Odessa said. "My magic's pretty weak at the moment, but I can get a boost from you, Storm."

"Sure. I'm fully charged."

I looked around my already messed up living room. Things couldn't get much worse by summoning the ghost back. "Let me grab a crystal ball and some candles from Magda's cabinet."

We settled in a circle on the floor and joined hands. The candle in the center ignited, and I positioned the crystal ball in front of it to amplify the ghost's energy so we could communicate. We all said the evoking chant.

The lights dimmed in the room, and the air chilled.

"It's working," Odessa whispered. "The ghost is coming back."

I kept my surprise hidden that it had worked so quickly. It wasn't my magic summoning the ghost. Odessa and Storm were doing the heavy lifting with this summoning.

The candle flame turned purple, indicating the ghost had arrived.

Odessa nudged me. "You ask the questions. He'll remember you."

"And remember how that turned out," I said.

"Go on," she encouraged.

I cleared my throat. "Spirit, why have you attached yourself to Luna?"

"The moon is lunar." The voice was barely a whisper. Perhaps the ghost trap had weakened him. Excellent. I could handle a weak ghost.

"I'm not asking you about the moon. I'm asking you about Luna Brimstone. You invaded her home and attacked her. Why do you wish to harm her?"

"It's my home."

"You lived in the apartment before Luna?" If that was true, it would be easy to find out who the previous tenants were.

"It's not right. A young girl living on her own."

"Why should that bother you?" I said. "Did you know Luna when you were alive?"

"It's not proper."

I looked at Storm and Odessa. "Something's off. The ghost I met cared nothing for Luna or her living situation."

"This ghost is talking like something out of the nineteenth century where women were supposed to be ladies and it was frowned upon to be unmarried," Storm said. "You don't think you caught the wrong ghost?"

"There wasn't more than one ghost in the apartment," Odessa said.

"There could have been," I said. "We were only focused on the one I made contact with. Luna said there'd been several ghosts living there when she looked around."

"What's your name, spirit?" Storm said.

The ghost didn't respond.

"We can send you on," Odessa said. "If you need help to leave, we can offer that. You just need to answer our questions. We're trying to keep our friend safe. Did you hurt her?"

"I saw what happened. She deserved it," the ghost said.

"No one deserves to be attacked and drained of their magic," I said. "Was it you?"

The ghost simply laughed.

"This is getting us nowhere," Storm said. "Let's blast this spirit out of existence. Maybe that'll fix things with Luna."

"No blasting," the ghost whispered.

"I need to see this ghost," I said. "I have a bad feeling we caught the wrong spirit. The voice sounds different."

"A reveal spell should work," Storm said.

A wave of light-headedness hit me. If I didn't stop trying magic soon, I'd pass out.

Odessa gave my hand a squeeze. "You sit this one out. We'll do the spell. Have another cookie and take a breather."

Storm narrowed her eyes at me, then nodded. "We've got this."

I eased back from the circle, feeling giddy and sick as I left them to the magic. My days of being a powerful witch were like a dream, almost like I'd been a different person. It felt like I'd never get my powers back. That was probably for the best, but at the moment, I was worse than useless.

"He's manifesting," Odessa whispered.

A wispy, indistinct image of an old man in a stiff collared shirt, his hair scraped off his face, appeared. He scowled at me.

I sighed and shook my head. "This is a different ghost."

"Did you see the ghost in Luna's apartment?" Odessa said.

"Not clearly, but whenever he manifested, he looked like a beast with glowing eyes and claws. This is just a little old man."

The ghost glared at me and jabbed a finger in my direction. "Less of the old. Respect your elders."

"You said you saw what happened to Luna," Odessa said. "Do you know who attacked her?"

The ghost drifted over to Odessa. "A bad spirit. One not to be trusted."

"You know who it is?" I asked.

He shook his head. "I want to leave. Help me to leave."

"This is a waste of time," Storm said. "Let's send away the old guy."

"I'll help you," Odessa said. "Focus on the candlelight and head toward it. Don't think about anything else. Just imagine yourself at peace, in the quiet, and happy."

"I haven't rested for a long time," the ghost said. "I lost my way. I was waiting for my wife. She's late for everything."

"You'll find her," Odessa said. "Just keep concentrating on the light. That's it."

The ghost drifted closer to the candle flame, until he appeared to slide inside it, and then he was gone. The candle returned to its normal color.

What a waste of time. We'd gotten nowhere in solving Luna's problem. All we'd done was deal with an old man with an attitude.

I grabbed the candle and stood. "I'm done. I can't help Luna."

"You are helping," Odessa said. "You saw the ghost that hurt her, and you've just helped another ghost. We're making progress."

"I was lucky not to be killed by the ghost when I confronted him," I said. "I don't have the power to deal with this trouble."

"You have power. Although it was lucky when Olympus caught you," Odessa said.

"Back up a few steps. What did I miss?" Storm said.

"I got slung out the window by the ghost we were supposed to trap."

"And that gorgeous guy from the Magic Council, Limpy Duke, caught her in his arms. He saved her life," Odessa said. "It was amazing."

"It was humiliating. And it shows he's following me around. I need to be more careful. The Magic Council is watching me. If I make too many wrong moves, I'll be back in magical rehab." I flexed my fingers. "Not that I've got much magic left to lose."

"You're definitely not running on full steam," Storm said. "But that doesn't mean you should quit."

"I'm not quitting anything. I'm just focusing on what I came here for. I should never have gotten involved." I slammed down the candle. "I'm not here to help Luna. She came to me. I didn't chase after her. She's the one who made the mistake. Why should I have to clear up her mess?"

"Because she was once your best friend," Odessa said. "You must still care for her."

"Or has all that dark magic addled your brain?" Storm said. "Maybe there's nothing left of the old Indigo."

"You're right. There isn't. It's time you both left. There are things I need to do."

Storm climbed to her feet. "Fine by me. I'm busy, too."

Odessa stepped in between us, a cookie held in each hand. "Rather than fighting, let's do something useful."

"I'm not going on another ghost hunt," I said.

"Agreed. So, let's visit Luna and see how she's doing." Odessa shoved a cookie in my mouth.

I took a bite. Yum, it was dark chocolate and orange. I looked around the room. I had to get on with clearing the house.

"Or have you quit your friendship with Luna, too?" Storm grabbed the cookie from Odessa.

I glared at her. "I'm not a quitter."

"Then let's go cheer up our friend." Odessa patted us both on the cheek.

I huffed out a breath. "Half an hour, then I'm done."

"Quitter," Storm muttered.

I flung a piece of cookie at her. She caught it and tossed it to Nugget, a smirk on her face.

I'd show her. I'd make a success of my time in Witch Haven. I'd sell this house, make a ton of money, and never see anyone from here ever again.

Chapter 12

Neither Storm nor I spoke much as we made our way to the hospital. I didn't appreciate being called a quitter. Why would no one listen to me when I said I couldn't take on this fight? Firstly, it wasn't my problem to deal with, and secondly, I wasn't equipped to take down this ghost. They could sense how weak my magic was, but they kept on pushing.

And although I didn't fear getting into more trouble with the Magic Council, their punishments weren't fun, and there was no way I wanted to go back into magical rehab. I was still recovering from the last time.

We walked through the main entrance of the small hospital set at the edge of the village and headed to the reception desk.

"She's in room twelve," Odessa said after she'd spoken to the nurse on duty. "This way." She skipped along in front of us.

I glanced at Storm. "It's best if I don't hang around for much longer. And I know you don't want me here."

She shrugged. "Stay or go, I don't care. I have bigger issues to deal with."

"Like what?"

"You'd know if you'd been here." She increased her pace.

I frowned at her back as I let her get some distance from me. Had Storm forgotten I'd had no choice but to leave?

Her rejection stung more than it should. Although I'd always been closest to Luna, Odessa and Storm had been good friends too, and we'd usually hang out at least once a week. Storm had always been on the sharp side, but back then I'd appreciated her honesty. I didn't appreciate it now.

"It's this room." Odessa knocked on the door and then walked in.

I failed to hide my grimace when I saw how pale Luna was. She was propped up on pillows behind her, a sheet covering her legs. She had dark circles under her eyes and her cheeks looked sunken.

I pushed away the guilt that gnawed at my stomach. I hadn't done this to Luna. She'd gone after the ghost on her own. This wasn't my fault, even though it felt like it was.

"Hey, you're looking really good. Better than the last time I visited. Is it all the gorgeous doctors making you feel better?" Odessa kissed Luna's cheek.

"You always were a terrible liar." Luna's voice was barely a whisper. "It's good to see you all. It's nice to see the gang back together."

I gave Luna's hand a squeeze. "It's like I've never been away. How are you feeling?"

She tilted her head from side to side. "Tired. I have no energy. The doctor can't detach the ghost from me. He keeps draining me."

"Who needs doctors when you have your friends? We're working on fixing your ghost problem," Odessa said.

"You are? Do you know what he wants with me?"

"Not yet. But we caught the ghost, so the mystery is almost solved."

"You captured him?" A weak smile appeared on Luna's face. "I don't feel any different. When did you get him?"

"Odessa," I muttered. "We haven't fixed things yet."

"He escaped before we could figure out what to do with him," Storm said.

I was surprised she hadn't dumped me in it by revealing I'd been the one to lose the ghost.

"Oh! I wondered why I wasn't feeling any better. If you'd taught him a lesson, he'd have let me go right away." Luna sighed and closed her eyes. "He's a strong ghost."

"We'll get him again," Odessa said. "He just surprised us. And we're still figuring out how to get rid of him completely."

Luna let out a soft sigh, a slight wheeze in her chest. "I'm grateful for anything you can do. I've never felt so cold before, and all I want to do is sleep. It feels like I'm aging about ten years every day. I must have done something terrible to get all this attention from such a nasty spirit."

I shook my head. "There's nothing bad about you. You always were the good one in the group. You

131

never broke curfew, always did your homework on time, and you didn't even sneak out on dates with unsuitable guys like all of us did."

"You're the regular goody two shoes of the group," Storm said.

Luna ducked her head. "I don't know about that. And things change. Something must have gone wrong. Otherwise, why am I being haunted?"

"The ghost said something about you having secrets. Does that make any sense?" I asked.

Luna's forehead wrinkled. "He's haunting me because of a secret I'm keeping?"

"I'm not sure. But is there anything you need to get off your chest?"

"No, it's bad luck, that's all," Odessa said. "The ghost could have been in that apartment when you moved in. He took a liking to you and now won't leave you alone."

"I'm not hiding anything that should make a ghost angry. I just don't think he likes me at all," Luna said. "I should have moved out as soon as I realized there was a problem, but it's such a beautiful apartment."

"And it's free," Storm said, a wicked gleam in her eyes.

Luna's cheeks flushed. "The rent's very reasonable. I got a great deal. I've been saving up for my own place, and my uncle's not getting any younger, and he'll retire soon. I want money to invest in the business when I take over. I've got so many plans, and they cost money. I was an idiot to put up with this ghost, but I didn't think it would get this bad."

"You aren't an idiot. You're planning for your future." Odessa perched on the edge of Luna's bed. "Once we get rid of this ghost, you can move back into your apartment and enjoy all the luxuries. It's your home. You won't be driven out."

Storm pulled out her phone. She flicked her fingers across the screen. "I need to leave. Duty calls." She patted Luna on the shoulder. "Don't go dying on us now."

"I'll do my best not to." Luna's smile looked weak as Storm left the room.

"Why's Storm always rushing off?" I said. "She raced off when we went to your apartment. I thought she didn't want to see the ghost."

Odessa and Luna exchanged a glance.

"What am I missing?" I said.

"You weren't here when her sister vanished," Odessa said.

"Eden's gone missing?"

Odessa nodded. "It happened five years ago. She was taken in the middle of the night. Whoever did it, snuck into the house, and took her out of her bed."

"Any idea who grabbed her?" I said.

"There were no clues left behind, just a faint residual of dark magic lingering in the air."

"No ransom note or message? Nothing to say what was going on?"

"Nope. It was like something evil be-spelled Eden away," Luna said.

"The Storm family never had anything to do with dark magic while I lived here. Did something change?" I said.

"Not that we know of," Odessa said. "The whole family was questioned, but they had no idea who'd want to take Eden. She was always a sweet girl."

"Is that why Storm changed careers?" I said. "When I was last here, she wanted to be a doctor."

Luna nodded, her eyelids drooping. "And she was for a while. She did the training, got the qualifications, and was working a residency here when it happened."

"Storm quit her job and set up a private investigation firm because she wasn't happy with how the Magic Council were investigating the case," Odessa said. "To begin with, she was only looking for her sister and learning from a mentor how to follow leads. That was all she cared about."

"Which is no surprise," I said.

Odessa nodded. "She was so close to Eden. Storm followed every lead and traveled hundreds of miles when someone got in touch and said they'd seen Eden. But she had to start earning money, so took other jobs on the side. She still goes after any lead linked to her sister, though. She's never given up hope that she'll find her one day."

I puffed out a breath. "It's a long time to have hope. Eden's been gone for years. Was there an ex-boyfriend on the scene causing trouble?"

"Eden dated a bit, but there was no one serious. The guys she dated were questioned, but they had alibis, and they all helped search for her. The whole village turned out to look for her. Everyone was devastated when she vanished."

"I bet. I liked Eden." I shook my head. "It seems like dark magic is messing with Witch Haven more and more."

Another look passed between Odessa and Luna.

"Is there a problem in the village?" I asked.

"We started having issues after you and your stepmom ran into... trouble," Odessa said.

I grimaced. "You don't have to sugar-coat it. We went rogue, killed a load of people, and severely messed up."

"Yes, that's what I meant." Odessa shuffled about on the bed. "Since then, there's been an increase in the amount of dark magic seeping into the village."

"Seeping in? There's an outside force doing this?" I didn't like where this conversation was going.

"Maybe. Although some people think you opened a doorway for it to enter," Luna said. "We don't believe that, but there has been a rise in the presence of dark magic since then."

"You think this is my fault?" A shudder ran down my spine. Had I opened the door to dark magic? Witch Haven had always been a peaceful place when I was growing up. It didn't seem that way any longer. Had I left behind the worst kind of legacy?

"No! No, I'm sure this has nothing to do with you." Odessa didn't look at me. "Almost positive. Eighty percent sure. Maybe fifty. Evens it's a coincidence."

"Yes! It could be a sign of the times," Luna said. "Magic is always shifting. Sometimes the good guys get control, and sometimes the bad guys get to have fun."

Unease shifted through me. All of this felt wrong. I should never have come back. What if me being here only made things worse? I should have left Magda's things and the house, and turned my back on it all. My life hadn't been so bad. Sure, it had been lonely, and it always felt weird, having my magic restrained by the Magic Council, but I was getting by. Now I was here, and everything felt thrown up in the air. I hated that feeling.

"Let's focus on getting this ghost back," Odessa said. "I can reinforce the magic traps and we can try again. We should go back to the apartment and see if he's returned there. Or if he hasn't—"

"I can't help anymore," I said.

"You must!" Odessa said. "We're so close to catching this ghost and making sure Luna gets better."

"We're really not. And I'm running out of time. I was only planning on being here for three days so I could clear Magda's house. That's all the time the Magic Council allowed me. After that, I'm leaving."

"Oh! I didn't know you were going so soon." Luna sounded croaky and feeble. "Do you have to go? I just got my friend back, and I like having you around. I don't want you to leave me again."

That felt like a dagger in the gut. "You should. After everything I did the last time I was here."

Luna beckoned me closer to the bed. "Stay. It feels like old times now you're back."

I didn't want to stay. This felt massively out of my comfort zone. I wanted a quiet life again. Tackling a violent ghost was the last thing I should get involved in. But one look at Luna's tear-filled eyes, and I couldn't say no to her.

136

"I'll try to stay a few more days. I'll see if I can negotiate something with the Magic Council. No guarantees."

Luna blinked away her tears. "I'd like that. I like having you around."

"And we can definitely help fix up the house," Odessa said. "With all of us helping, you'll have it cleared in no time. Then you can decide what you want to do next."

I nodded. The extra help would be useful, and even though I wasn't staying, I needed to get the place fixed up so I could sell it and pay the debts. "Okay, some help to get the house tidy would be good."

There was a knock on the door, and it was pushed open.

I turned and frowned at the sight of Olympus looming in the doorway.

Luna sat up in the bed, shooting me a worried look. "Hello. Can we help you?"

He stepped into the room, his attention on me. "Indigo Ash, you're under arrest."

Chapter 13

"You can't arrest Indigo. She's done nothing wrong." Luna struggled to get out of bed.

I placed a restraining hand on her arm. "Stay where you are. You need to rest."

"They can't take you away, you've been helping me."

Olympus walked closer, all brooding and superior. "You need to come with me. And come quietly. This is a hospital."

"Why are you arresting Indigo?" Odessa stood from the bed and came to my side. She wrapped an arm around my waist.

"For her illegal use of magic."

"She hasn't been doing anything like that," Odessa said. "Indigo's power is restrained. She can't use strong spells. I know because I've been around her most of the time."

"Do you deny that you summoned a spirit in your stepmom's house?" Olympus said to me.

I gritted my teeth. How did he know about that? It was most likely the trolls snooping. "What if I did?"

"Was it the spirit who injured Luna you brought forward?"

"We had everything under control," Odessa said. "There were three of us there. We know what we're doing."

"How did you plan to subdue a dangerous, out-of-control malevolence?" Olympus said.

Odessa glanced at me as she fidgeted with her hair. "We're strong witches."

"So you had no idea what you were doing," Olympus said. "Indigo knows the rules. She cannot use spells above a certain level. She's also aware that summoning a negative force breaks the terms of her probation."

Odessa looked at me and bit her bottom lip. "I didn't know that. You should have said."

I shook my head. "We were trying to help Luna. We needed to make contact with the ghost to find out what he wanted."

"You're admitting you broke your terms of probation?" Olympus said.

"Limpy! It was for a really good cause," Odessa said.

"My name is Olympus. Do you want me to arrest you, too?"

"For using a cute nickname on you? I don't think that charge will stick, but you can always try." Odessa batted her lashes at him. "Luna has to get better, and until we figure out what's going on with this ghost, she'll be stuck in here wasting away to nothing."

Luna ducked her head. "I hope it won't come to that, but I do feel terrible."

I glanced at Luna. She was gray and sweaty. We had to do something about this ghost, or there was a real chance she'd die.

"Let's move," Olympus said to me.

Odessa stepped between us and fluttered her lashes at him again. "This is a simple misunderstanding. Why don't you drop by my farm and you can pick whatever pumpkins you like? I'll even throw in a free scarecrow. Mine are top of the range, and I guarantee a crow free yard. They're hard-working and reliable."

"Bribery won't work on me," Olympus said.

"Don't think of it as bribery. This is me making sure our magic enforcers are always well-fed and have no problems with crows," Odessa said.

"I'll pass. Indigo, will you come quietly, or do I have to make this arrest formal?"

I tugged Odessa out of the way. She could offer free pumpkins for a year, and he wouldn't budge on this matter. "I'll come with you."

"That's the most sensible decision you've made since you've been here," he said. "Let's get this over with."

"What's going to happen to her?" Luna said. "You're not sending Indigo back to prison, are you?"

"That's what usually happens when someone breaks their parole," Olympus said.

Odessa and Luna talked over each other, protesting my innocence and saying it wasn't fair.

I waved a hand at them until they were quiet. "I'll deal with it. I knew what I was doing when I used that magic."

"Then you're a fool. We're always watching you," Olympus said. "You're one of the most dangerous witches we've ever had to deal with."

"We'll get you out as quickly as we can," Odessa said. "And if you need us to testify about your character, just ask."

"That won't help. We already know what her character is like." Olympus gestured to the door. "This way, Indigo."

I trudged ahead of Olympus, along the corridor and out of the hospital. I should have stuck to my original plan and not gotten involved with helping Luna.

"Where are we going?" I said.

"I have a temporary office here. You can answer my questions when we get there."

"You set up a special office just because I was in the village?"

He smirked. "You've made a reputation for yourself. That's gotten you noticed."

"I'm almost flattered."

"Don't be. It's a terrible reputation."

I glanced at him. "All you care about is what I did wrong. Until I came back here, I hadn't put a foot out of line. I was trying to live my life, keep my head down, and not get in any trouble."

"I know. We've had tabs on you ever since you got out. And I've been monitoring your weekly therapy sessions."

It shocked me he'd been paying such close attention. "So you know this is a one-off. I tried to stay out of Luna's problems, but we used to be good friends. And... I owe her."

141

"I also know that."

"Is there anything you don't know about me? What's my favorite color? Do I have a favorite flavor of ice cream? What side of the bed do I sleep on?"

His gaze ran over me. "Probably black, I'd go for rocky road, and you sleep on the left side."

I turned and stared at him. "Purple. I hate all ice cream. And yes, I do sleep on the left side. How did you know that?"

"I had a fifty-fifty chance of getting it right." Olympus slid a glance my way. "I should have guessed about the purple, considering the color of your hair. Although what's the deal with the ice cream hating?"

"I get brain freeze and a weird aftertaste. I like eating it, but I always get this gone off milk taste in my mouth afterward. Now, if you want to treat me to 'nice' cream, it's a date."

"I've never heard of it."

"It's dairy free. You mix up fruit, sweetener, and peanut butter, stir it all up, stick it in the freezer, and you have all the yummy goodness without the aftertaste or the calories."

"Huh! You learn something new every day."

"If you really knew me, you'd know I didn't come here to cause trouble. I really came to sort out Magda's things. And only after you forced me to come back because you want to get paid."

"I didn't have a hand in that."

"You run the Magic Council."

"I chair the head committee. All decisions happen by democratic agreement."

"That sounds like a lot of hot air. You're in charge."

142

"Only of some things."

"So you're not here out of choice? Who made you come here?"

He hesitated. "It was my choice to ensure your visit went smoothly."

That stopped me for a second. Olympus Duke had a personal interest in me. I wasn't sure whether to be scared or curious. "And it would have been smooth if a ghost wasn't after my best friend."

"Yet you still got involved, knowing it would take you along the wrong path."

"Because Luna's a friend. At least she was." I tipped my head back. "Maybe I should have ignored her problem. What would you do if your best friend reached out and asked for help?"

Olympus stopped by a small office set back off the main road and unlocked it. "Probably the same as you. This way."

I walked in ahead of him into a compact open plan office. The only furniture in there were two chairs, a table, and a cabinet. On top of the cabinet was a kettle and some paperwork.

"Take a seat," he said. "Do you want anything to drink?"

"I'll take the largest glass of rum punch you've got."

"I meant coffee."

"I'll pass. Let's get this over with." I perched on the edge of a seat. I couldn't figure out how to get out of this. I had broken the rules, and I knew what I'd been doing, but I just haven't been able to turn my back on my old friend.

I tapped my feet on the floor as Olympus took his time making a coffee for himself.

"Are you sure you don't want one?" He held out the mug.

"Positive. How bad will this be for me?"

"That's not for me to decide. I'm here to gather the relevant information." He sat in the seat opposite me, sat back and took a sip of coffee. He placed several pages in front of him. "Tell me about your visit to Luna's apartment."

"There's not much to tell. You already know she's been having problems with a ghost. I went there to see if I could get rid of it."

"What did you find?"

"An aggressive spirit with an attitude. He wants Luna as his plaything, and he's not letting her go."

"I'm guessing you weren't happy about that."

"You guessed right. I tried to reason with him, but as you know, he tossed me out the window and I landed on top of you."

"And I have the bruises and jarred back to prove it."

"You have my undying gratitude." I narrowed my eyes. "I did appreciate it. My magic wouldn't have saved me."

"I was doing my job. I have to protect people from danger." He shifted the papers in front of him. "I've followed your case with interest. What happened with Magda has never made sense to me."

"You're not the only one who is flummoxed. But why the interest?"

"I want to know why you did it."

"Killed sixty-six people?"

"Yes. There has to be more to the story."

"No. The story is complete. My stepmom got in over her head with dark magic, it infected me because I was living with her, and we decided to have some fun." I didn't meet his gaze. I'd never been able to explain what happened that day and still woke drenched in sweat as my subconscious replayed the horror of what went down.

"You're an Ash witch. Your biological mom was one of the strongest witches ever to have lived in Witch Haven."

"I don't see your point."

"You should have been strong enough to resist dark magic. You can control the elements."

"I wish I had answers for you. Maybe I'm not as strong as my mom. Besides, she wasn't all powerful. After all, she died giving birth to me."

Olympus shook his head. "Which was a tragedy. And your dad died five years after marrying Magda?"

"He did. And she took me in as her own. But Dad never got over losing my mom, and even when he remarried Magda, he wasn't truly happy."

"He admitted that?"

"No! Not to me, but I was his daughter. I could tell he was sad. So could Magda, and she tried so hard to make him happy."

"She looked after you?"

"She did. Magda was a great stepmom. There was nothing wicked about her. I don't know what changed her, but it happened so quickly." I shifted in the seat. "Anyway, we're not here to talk about my family."

K.E. O'CONNOR

"We are. It's relevant. It may help me understand why you went rogue."

"I messed up. I made a mistake. I lost my way with magic. Is that not enough of an explanation?"

Olympus tapped one finger on the table. "It'll have to be for now."

I sat up straight. I didn't want any more chats about my family. It was none of his business. They were all dead. I didn't want him dragging up painful memories because he was on some crusade to bolster his already huge reputation in the Magic Council.

"So, you don't deny using magic to summon the spirit?" Olympus said.

"You know I did, so there's no point in denying it."

"And you know the terms of your probation. You broke them."

I nodded, a coldness settling in the pit of my stomach. "I understand. What happens next?"

"Lucky for you, Judge Zimmerman is out of the area. He's coming to Witch Haven in three days. He'll be the one to pass sentence on you."

"Have you any idea what that sentence might be?"

"I have a good idea."

"Do you care to share the good news?"

He was quiet for a few seconds. "You'll lose what's left of your magic."

An ache radiated out from my middle. "You'll turn me into a shadow?"

"Maybe it should have happened after you killed all those people, but you got the benefit of the doubt because of your age. You've shown you can't control yourself as soon as you're around magic. There have to be consequences."

"But... but where will I go? No one will want me if I have no magic. I'll be an outcast in the magic community." I also wouldn't fit in anywhere else. Magic users drained of all power give off a vibe that makes other non-magic users shy away from them. They don't know what the problem is, but they don't want to be around you. I'd be a freak wherever I went. I'd find nowhere to call home.

Olympus looked away. "I don't make the rules."

"You could bend them to help me. Is there another option? More rehab? I'll take that."

A flicker of indecision passed across his face. He shook his head. "You've been through rehab. It failed."

"Consider putting in a good word for me. I didn't fight you when you ordered me to come here. I'm behaving. I'm being a good little witch."

"Only because you got caught. What would you have gone on to next?"

I sighed. I had been planning on ghost hunting and destroying the thing messing with Luna. That would have involved using powerful magic. "I guess it doesn't matter now."

Olympus looked down at the papers in front of him. "This is out of my hands."

"Of course it is. There's no reason you'd want to help me, even if you could."

His eyes narrowed as he looked up at me. "I admired the Ash witches."

"If that's true, then how about you let that admiration do me one tiny favor?"

147

"You're in no position to request favors."

"Call it a soon to be shadow witch's last request. I'll forego my final meal if you do this for me."

He pursed his lips. "What is it?"

"I'll accept my punishment, whatever it is, but since the judge won't be here for three days, give me an extension so I can sort out Magda's house. I can get it cleared in that time. The Magic Council want their money. If I get it on the market, whatever it sells for, it's all yours. My debt to you will be paid. Doesn't money always make the Magic Council happy?"

"Keeping the world safe from rogue supernaturals makes us happy."

"You're not a tiny bit interested in the cash? That house will fetch a great price."

"Not with its dark past."

"Everyone loves a little danger in their lives."

He snorted a laugh. "That won't work. Besides, the decision has changed regarding what will happen to your stepmom's house."

I glared at him. "When were you going to tell me about this change?"

"I'm telling you now. The house has been scheduled to be destroyed at midnight tonight."

My cheeks burned and my eyes blurred with angry tears. "You can't do that! All Magda's things are still in there. I haven't had a chance to move anything out. And her familiars live there. You can't destroy the house with them inside."

"They'll be moved out, so long as we can find them."

148

I pressed a hand against my stomach, not sure whether I wanted to puke or scream. "At least let me get back in there so I can grab what I can carry."

"That's not happening either. You're staying under the Magic Council's custody from now on. You can't be trusted."

"You're locking me up?"

He nodded. "I have a space here that's suitable."

"Was that your decision?"

"It was a joint decision. It's to ensure the safety of the village. You must understand the risk you pose."

I sank into the chair and closed my eyes. I understood just fine. I was speeding along on an out-of-control broomstick, which was on fire, while an enraged dragon chased me toward an angry hoard of gremlins, and there was nothing I could do to stop the collision. My time as a witch was almost over, and I was about to lose everything.

Chapter 14

The night had felt painfully long as I'd lain on the single bed in the room Olympus had left me in. I say room, but it was a cell, just without the physical bars. There were plenty of magic wards to stop me breaking out and causing trouble.

I'd watched the time as it ticked closer to midnight. I'd had to force myself not to cry as it hit that fated number, and the house I'd been raised in was destroyed by the Magic Council. All the history and knowledge gathered by Magda was reduced to rubble. It was such a waste.

Why could no one see there had once been a good witch living there? They only judged her on the last few weeks of her life. And sure, those weeks had been the worst imaginable, but Magda hadn't always been bad. And neither had I.

It was barely past dawn, and I'd been awake for a couple of hours. The room was dull, with only a small window at the top to let in light.

I was bored, angry, and just a little furious with the world. I also had nothing to lose if I broke a few more rules. So I cast a light spell.

I didn't expect it to work, given the wards surrounding me muted magic, so I was surprised when a near-perfect ball of light formed over my head.

That had been too easy. My magic never worked that well these days.

I cast another one, and it did the exact same thing.

A mild warning from the wards tingled against my skin, but I ignored it. When I cast spells these days, they went wrong. So what had changed?

It should be harder in here to get any magic to activate, but I'd barely felt the impact of casting those spells.

I sat up and ran through a list of basic spells I'd been taught when I was younger. A light spell, a warmth spell, and a protection spell. They all worked. What was going on?

I climbed off the bed and peered out the window in the door. No one was around to sense I was doing anything wrong. After Olympus had locked me in, he'd disappeared. I figured he'd gone home to celebrate catching the evil witch of Witch Haven.

I turned, blocking the window so no one could see in, and cast the first elemental spell I'd tried since I'd gotten out of prison.

A gentle breeze floated around the cell, lightly kissing my skin, before vanishing.

"No way," I whispered. I shouldn't be able to do that. Controlling the elements was beyond my current powers.

I looked at my hands. My magic didn't feel at full-strength, but that was most likely because of the wards. But it was there, simmering beneath the surface.

I'd doubted my ability to cast reliable spells for such a long time that I always expected them to go wrong.

Maybe there was something to be said for being careful what you wished for because it could come true. I'd just wanted to be invisible, and it had happened, along with my ability to cast magic.

But I did notice a shift in my magic when I joined energies with Odessa and Storm. I'd ignored it at the time, so certain that I'd fail. Could that be the reason my power was working again?

I was used to doing things on my own and muddling through, that I'd forgotten what it felt like to join energies with other witches. It always intensified the power of spells.

I shook my head. Even if my magic liked being here, it was too complicated to remain in Witch Haven. I couldn't stay.

A small tapping on the outside window had me raising my gaze. It was high up, so I couldn't see out, but it sounded like someone was outside.

I stood on my tiptoes and saw something black moving against the glass.

A dark shape flew past. Was that Russell? How did he know I was here?

Two long spidery limbs waggled at me through the glass.

A grin split my face. "Hilda, is that you?" I glanced behind me to make sure no one was in the corridor, then hurried over to the opposite wall. "Can you hear me? Tap if you can hear me."

There was louder tapping on the window.

I backed up again to see what she was doing. This time, Russell was perched next to her. He tapped his beak against the glass and lifted his head a couple of times.

A few seconds later, the glass splintered and blew inside.

I dodged just in time as it showered down beside me.

Russell wiggled through the gap, followed by Hilda, who abseiled down on a string of webbing.

Russell flew around me before settling on my shoulder.

Hilda ran up my leg and touched my hand. "We had to get you out. We heard what happened from Odessa when she came to the house and didn't think it was right."

"I appreciate the escape effort, but you'll get in trouble being here."

"We don't care," Hilda said.

Russell cawed his agreement.

"The Magic Council caught me breaking the rules. They're going to punish me."

"Did you fight your corner and tell them why you did it?" Hilda said.

"In a way, but I knew they wouldn't listen to me."

"You give up too easily." Nugget stood on the window ledge. "You never used to be such a quitter."

"You're not the first one to call me that since I got back here." Everyone seemed to know me better than I did. "I'm surprised you made the effort to break me out. I figured you'd be glad I was out of your fur."

"I was. And I still think you're an idiot, but you're our idiot, and we need to look out for you. Especially when you do stupid things and get caught by the Magic Council."

A laugh shot out of me. He'd called me an idiot, but I was his idiot, and it felt good to be wanted. "That's the best compliment you've given me since I got here."

"Stick around and I'll give you some more. But we need to get out of here, before someone notices a broken window and a magnificent magical cat silhouetted in the early morning light."

"Err... we have a problem. There are magic wards on the door, and I can't fit through that window," I said.

"You won't have to," Hilda said. "Russell, go deal with the lock and the wards."

Russell lifted off my shoulder and flapped in front of the lock, before jamming his beak inside. There was a shower of multi-colored sparks, and something clicked. He then dropped two red stones on the floor.

"You'd better stand back," Hilda said. "They're full of a diffusion spell. That always creates a lot of smoke."

I backed away as the stones hummed. Orange smoke filled the room, and the air buzzed with magical energy.

There was a pop, and the smoke vanished.

I hurried to the door and tried it. It opened easily. The wards were gone. "Wow! Russell, that was impressive. Nice job, my feathery gladiator."

He settled on my shoulder and tapped his beak against my head, before preening his feathers.

"I'll go ahead and make sure no one's around," Hilda said. "When I wave my legs at you, that means it's safe to move. When I freeze, you do the same." She scurried down my leg and out the door.

Nugget dropped to the floor and walked over to me.

"I'm still not sure this is a great idea," I said.

"I told them we shouldn't waste our time on you, but they never listen to me," Nugget said.

I risked ruffling the fur on his head. "I know you like me, really."

"I don't hate you." He flicked his tail. "Let's start with that."

I peeped out the doorway. Hilda was almost at the end of the corridor. She turned and waggled her legs.

"Unless you've gotten used to your new accommodation, let's get out of here," Nugget said.

There were only three other doors along the corridor, and I tiptoed past them until I reached Hilda. "Is there any sign of anyone from the Magic Council?" I whispered.

Hilda touched my leg. "The coast is clear. That's why we came early. We figured there'd only be a skeleton staff working. But we should hurry. If anyone notices there's something wrong with the magic wards, they'll check your room."

I propped open the door at the end of the corridor, wide enough for Hilda to get through and so I could see her progress.

She scuttled along for about thirty seconds and then froze.

A second later, two male voices filtered toward me.

I eased the door closed and backed away. I tried the other doors in the corridor, but they were locked. The only place I could hide was back in my room, and I didn't want to end up trapped in there with a broken window to explain. I ducked behind the main door and waited.

The voices grew fainter and then vanished.

I blew out a breath as I eased open the door again.

Hilda was on the move, heading away from us. She turned and waggled her legs.

Nugget went through first, and I took up the rear with Russell still perched on my shoulder.

Hilda froze again.

I was right by a door when she stopped moving. Although I had no idea what was on the other side, I yanked it open and stepped in. Nugget dashed in with me, and I was whacked in the face by a wet mop that had been stood up to dry.

I gagged and shoved it out of the way as the smell of bleach and dirty water filled my nose.

"Quiet," Nugget hissed. "You'll give away our location if you keep crashing into things."

I jabbed a finger at the filthy mop.

He gave a snort. "You should have looked where you were going."

I grabbed the door handle and held it. If someone tried this door, maybe they'd think it was locked and go away.

Footsteps stopped right outside, along with my heart.

I closed my eyes and pressed my lips together. This was it. We were about to get caught. My escape attempt would give the Magic Council another reason to take away all my magic. Not that they needed any more.

"Blast them with a spell," Nugget whispered.

I shook my head. No one was getting hurt because I was being an idiot and trying to escape.

The footsteps started up again, moving away from the door.

It felt like I hadn't breathed for a couple of minutes and was lightheaded as I eased open the door.

Hilda was right outside. "Let's go. We had a lucky escape. That was the janitor, but he was called away. We just have a small office to get through, and then we can escape out of the main door."

Olympus's voice hit my ears, and I tensed.

"Eek! Change of plan," Nugget said. "This way." He raced along the corridor in front of me with Hilda.

I sped after them, running on my tiptoes to make as little noise as possible. "Where are we going?"

"Out the back," Nugget said.

"There's a back way in?"

"Most likely. We just need to find it."

"You don't know? We could be heading along a dead end. What if there's only one way in and out of this building?"

"We're about to find that out," Nugget said.

157

I glanced over my shoulder, but no one was following us. I started trying random doors, hoping one led outside. I found two offices and another storage closet.

"I smell fresh air," Nugget said. "Follow me."

I shoved open another door and stumbled out into the early morning light. I eased the door shut behind me, then took a few seconds to get my bearings. We were in a back alley, and there were trash cans by the door we'd come out of.

No one else was around. It was still early and would be hours before the stores in the village opened. We'd done it. I was free, for now.

"Thanks for getting me out of there," I said.

"We're your familiars. We're always going to help you." Hilda had scuttled up my leg again and was touching the back of my hand. "Let's go home. You need rest and food. I expect they didn't look after you in there."

My stomach felt hollow as I shook my head. "Hilda, wait. All of you need to listen to me. You're not my familiars. I have no claim on you. And while I do appreciate the help, you're free to go where you like." I didn't want them getting attached to me. I had no worries about Nugget, he just about tolerated me, but Hilda and Russell were a concern.

"You're wrong. We're yours," Hilda said, a finality to her tone.

"No, you're not. And we don't have a home anymore," I said. "You must have seen the house get destroyed last night."

"We saw the Magic Council arrive," Hilda said.

A cold ache settled in my gut. They'd really gone through with destroying the house. There was a tiny part of my brain unwilling to believe it had happened. "Then I have no home here. And it's time to leave while I have the chance. The second Olympus knows I'm on the loose, he'll come after me."

Russell squawked and leaped off my shoulder.

"Shush! Keep the noise down. We're not out of danger yet. Let's get away from here," I said.

"Hey, not so fast. You're not going anywhere," Nugget said.

"We have to move! The second they realize the cell is empty, they'll come looking for me."

"Tell us your grand plan now we've gotten you free," Nugget said.

"I have to get out of Witch Haven. I can't stay. There's nothing here for me."

"You don't think there's anything here for you?" Hilda ran down my leg. "What about us?"

"You can't leave us," Nugget said. "We just saved you, and this is how you repay us? You're walking away?"

"I don't know what you want me to do. Give you a few cat treats as a thank you?"

Nugget snorted. "I knew this was a mistake. We wasted our time helping you, and now you're abandoning us."

"I'm not abandoning you. And until a few days ago, I didn't even know you all lived at the house. You'll find somewhere else to go. I can even help you look for a new place if you like."

159

"We don't want a new place," Nugget said. "We've got a home. We're happy there."

"If I don't go now, I'll be arrested."

Hilda shot out a long string of webbing, slid to the ground, and scuttled away.

"Hilda! I'm sorry. I didn't think you'd care about what I did," I said.

Russell gave another loud squawk and flew away.

"Look what you've done. You've upset Hilda and Russell," Nugget said.

"I didn't mean to. And I am grateful you got me out, but you have to see this makes sense. If I stay, I'm toast. The Magic Council are bringing in a judge to pass sentence on me. They're going to take all my magic. I'll be a shadow. I won't belong here. I won't belong anywhere."

Nugget hissed at me. "I don't see why that worries you. You like being an outcast."

"I don't! I've just... adjusted. I had no choice after what happened."

"You did. You chose to retreat from the world of magic. You acted like you had no ability left and wanted nothing to do with the community. You turned your back on us."

"Witch Haven turned its back on me. I don't blame them for doing that, but coming back here has shown me I made the right decision to stay away. As soon as I'm back, people get hurt."

"Of course, they get hurt. Life happens to us all. It's messy and complicated and sometimes causes problems. You just chose not to know about it. Luna's been in trouble with that ghost for a long time. You'd have known that if you'd reached out and made contact once you got out. Instead, you retreated to lick your wounds."

"They were big wounds," I said. "I deserved to have some downtime and look after myself."

He hissed again. "You should be ashamed of behaving that way. You're an Ash witch. They stand up for the defenseless."

"You don't know what you're talking about," I muttered.

"I do. Come with me. I'll show you exactly what you have to stay for." Nugget marched away along the alleyway.

I hesitated. I should go. The longer I stayed in Witch Haven, the bigger the risk I'd get caught. But I knew these familiars, and they had just helped me out. I owed them.

"What do you have to show me?" I hurried along behind Nugget.

"You'll see. It's worth staying for, but only if you're witch enough to handle it."

Chapter 15

"This is what you wanted to show me?" I stared at the huge pile of rubble. It was all that was left of Magda's house. "Are you rubbing my nose in everything I've lost?"

Nugget growled at me. "Stop acting like you don't have magic. Use what you've got left to see the truth. It's right in front of your eyes."

"I'm looking and I'm seeing. The Magic Council destroyed the house, just like they said they would."

Nugget headbutted me hard in the calf.

"I'm out of here. I shouldn't have wasted my time coming with you." I dodged out the way as Nugget charged me. "Hey! Quit thumping me. You have a bony head."

"You won't believe it until you can feel it." He rammed into me again.

"What am I supposed to feel, other than angry and frustrated?" I backed away from Nugget as he continued to headbutt me. I froze as something tingled up my spine. "What was that?"

"Finally! You're sensing it. If you weren't so convinced about how useless your magic was, you'd have felt it the second we got near."

I turned and held out my hands. Now I was paying attention, I sensed there was some kind of magic barrier in front of me, exactly where Magda's house used to be.

And it was huge. I spent ten minutes exploring how far it went.

I stepped back and stared at the pile of rubble to my right. "That's in the wrong place."

"Exactly. Because that rubble doesn't belong to your house," Nugget said.

"I still don't get it. What did you do?"

"Think about it. There's only one thing that needs a barrier spell as big as that."

I touched the boundary of the magic again, and its energy tingled on my skin. Excitement skittered through me. "The house is behind here?"

"We couldn't let the Magic Council take our home. When we heard what they planned to do, we got to work," Nugget said. "And it wasn't so hard. This house has a tendency to flip itself around when it's in the mood for a re-design. Convincing it to shift over didn't take long. This house wants to remain standing just as much as we want to keep living in it."

A smile hit me. "I remember! When I was a kid, the front door would move from one side to the other, and the rooms would rearrange themselves."

"You got it. We used the house's desire to change to conceal it. It took us hours to create a realistic enough replica to fool the Magic Council."

"You, Russell, and Hilda did this?"

"We did. In case you haven't noticed, we're awesome familiars." Nugget licked a paw and swiped it over an ear.

I nodded. I'd underestimated them and forgotten how powerful they were. "What happened when the Magic Council got here?"

"There were three guys who arrived at midnight. They were grumpy and tired and just wanted to get it done. They didn't do much checking, just fired up the spells and blasted the house to pieces."

"Didn't they go inside and check it was safe? They must have known about the powerful magic contained in the walls. And I told Olympus that you lived here and to make sure you all got out safely."

"They didn't bother about any of that," Nugget said. "Not that I'm surprised. Our association with you and Magda hasn't left us with the best reputations. They'd have been happy if we died when the house was destroyed."

I clenched my fists, anger bubbling inside me. "That's illegal. You can't destroy a familiar. It injures the witch they're connected to."

"That's probably another bonus reason to get rid of us. It would have kept you weak. Besides, they can kill a familiar who's lost their owner," Nugget said. "And you've made it clear you don't want us."

That made me feel like a total heel. "I... I honestly don't know what I want." I gestured at the concealed house. "I never expected my stepmom to die. I never expected to come back here. And I really never thought I'd end up in a position like this."

"Look at the positive. You still have the house, and all the power is still inside, just as it should be. It's yours, if you want it." Nugget walked to the magic barrier and placed his front paws against it.

The magic shivered, and a small opening appeared, revealing the house.

I walked closer, a smile on my face. I'd have missed this place if it was destroyed. "We'll have to keep the house concealed until we figure out how to keep it."

"And convince the Magic Council it doesn't need to be blown up," Nugget said.

I looked around to make sure no one was watching us. "What happened to the trolls?"

"Once the house was destroyed, they were sent away."

"We'll have to keep this barrier in place. We don't want the Magic Council to find out what we've done."

"So it's *we* now? You're planning on sticking around?"

I grimaced. I'd been a jerk to Nugget, Hilda, and Russell. I hadn't meant to lash out, but I was freakin' terrified. I didn't want to lose my magic, and I didn't want to lose this place.

I kneeled beside Nugget. "Thanks. For everything. I'm not the easiest person to be around at times."

"No kidding. You've been a horror since you returned to Witch Haven."

I could have argued with him, but he was right. "I don't know how long we'll get to keep this house, but you can stay as long as you like. All three of you. Your home is here."

"Of course, we will. It's always been our home." Nugget flicked his tail. "You may pet my head as your reward for finally coming to your senses."

"Petting you is my reward?"

"It is. I'm very soft. I spend hours a day grooming."

"With your tongue. And I know where else that goes."

"I'm clean! But only pet my head. You can tickle in between my ears and around my ruff, but if you touch my belly, back, or tail, you die."

I laughed and gave Nugget a tentative scratch between the ears. "Why did you do this?"

"I'm selfish. I don't want to move anywhere else. I have my bed just the way I like it. And now you're here, I'll get regular meals. I have a long list of things I prefer to eat. Tinned cat food isn't one of them. I like fresh tuna. Magda always made fresh."

"You purred loudly enough when I gave it to you."

"A starving cat will think moldy cheese and stale bread is tasty. I have much more refined tastes." He glanced at me. "Hilda and Russell kept going on about making sure you didn't lose your home and had something to stick around for, but that didn't bother me. You'll make your own decisions. We're not going to sway you. You left us behind a long time ago."

Nugget had a hard exterior, but it didn't take a genius to figure out I'd hurt him. I continued to tickle between his ears, and after a minute, he gave a quiet purr.

"I need to make it right with Russell and Hilda."

"You do. And they did the heavy lifting when concealing this house. I supervised, which is also

166

an important job. If there's no coordination, then there's chaos. You hurt their feelings when you said you were leaving."

"I hurt yours, too."

He nibbled on his leg. "I don't care what you do. But for some strange reason, they've grown attached to you."

I let out a sigh. "They shouldn't have bothered."

"That's what I keep telling them."

"And you're right. The world is better off without me. I can't offer people anything by coming back to Witch Haven."

"I agree."

"So, what do I do?"

"Beats me. But when you sell the house, make sure you put a condition in the deeds to say we have to stay. If a witch takes it on, we can assess her to see if she's good enough for us. We could even become her familiars since you don't want us."

I wish I could keep them as mine. "You're all amazing familiars. Any witch would be grateful to have you."

He was quiet for a few seconds. "But not you."

"I would, but it's complicated."

"It always is with you. And that's of your own choosing. It's just a pity you're not witch enough to take this on."

I looked at the house. "If things were different, if the Magic Council weren't hunting me, I'd stay."

"You don't owe me an explanation. I was around when things went bad. I may even have turned tail and run myself if I'd committed such atrocities."

My mouth went dry as my past threatened to overwhelm me. "I can't change the past, but I can change the present."

Nugget tilted his head. "You're staying?"

I nodded. "For now. We'll have to be sneaky to ensure the Magic Council don't find out you fooled them and catch me. I'll figure out how to sell this house and make sure you're all safe and have a home for as long as you need."

"Or you could try figuring out if there's a permanent place for you in Witch Haven," Nugget said.

"That's impossible."

"I disagree. But you do have the quitter label firmly attached to you, so I won't be surprised when you abandon us."

"I'm not a..." maybe I was throwing in the towel too quickly. But I had good reason. "I have the small matter of being an escaped prisoner to deal with."

"It's a challenge, but it could be worth it."

I took a long look at the house. My home. "I didn't think you liked me."

"I didn't say I did, but Hilda and Russell would be upset if you left. I hate it when they're miserable."

I stared through the gap in the magic barrier. Was there a life for me here? A community I could be a part of? For the first time in a long time, I felt excited about my future.

But before I could puzzle through that conundrum, I had bridges to mend. "Let's get out of here. We need to find Hilda and Russell. I owe them big time."

Three hours later, my feet were aching and my options gone. "I don't know how I'll persuade them to come back." I ducked out from behind a building as we continued our fruitless search for Hilda and Russell.

"I suggest a six course meal, the room of their choice in the house, and you to be their slave for a month," Nugget said.

"I don't even know what a six course meal for a spider would involve," I said.

"Lots of flies. Hilda's great at getting rid of those. She's also partial to chocolate. Russell likes fruit and crickets. You should catch them yourself to show extra effort." Nugget was trotting beside me, being surprisingly cheerful.

"What do you want out of this deal?" We'd been sneaking around Witch Haven all morning trying to find my missing familiars, and done several circuits of the village, risking getting spotted every time we moved.

"I'm thinking about it. But it's time for my nap. We can keep looking later." Nugget strode away, leaving me hiding behind a bush.

I checked the coast was clear, before scurrying after him. "We still haven't found Hilda and Russell. What if they've left the village?"

"To go where? They've only ever known this place."

I nudged Nugget into the tree line that ran along the road. He was terrible at keeping a low profile. "We could try behind the stores again. The alleyways are a great place to hide."

"You check the trash cans if you like. I need to recharge."

We were taking a huge risk by searching in the daytime, but I was keen to make amends.

"We'll start again at dusk," I said.

"That works with my feeding, napping, and grooming schedule."

I slowed as we approached the magical barrier concealing the house. My eyes widened, and I groaned. Russell and Hilda sat on the pile of rubble, looking gloomy.

"You're here!" I dashed over to them. "We've been looking for you."

Hilda lifted one long black leg, and I touched it.

"We came by an hour ago," she said.

"I'm sorry. I didn't mean to make you unhappy. This is your home. You're welcome to stay as long as you like."

Hilda turned to Russell, and he flapped his wings.

"And the rest," Nugget said.

I raised my hand. "I owe you. How about a meal on me? Whatever you like."

"Say how many courses," Nugget said.

"Six? Yes, six courses. Of whatever you want."

Hilda waggled her front legs. "That sounds nice."

"And...." Nugget said.

"Your rooms! You can both have a whole room to yourselves. Whichever one you like. I want to make it up to you. I shouldn't have shoved you away. I was a jerk, and I was scared about what was happening to me."

"That's very generous of you," Hilda said.

Russell squawked and flapped his wings again.

"So, you're all staying?" I asked.

"I'm in," Nugget said.

Russell bobbed his head up and down.

Hilda waggled her legs. "Me, too. And just so you know, I'd have come back without you throwing in all the sweeteners. You're not a bad witch, Indigo. You'd be an amazing witch if you put your mind to it."

Russell squawked and flew around my head a few times, before zipping through the magic barrier and over to the house.

"Great. Let's get inside so you can pick out your rooms." I stepped through the front door and let out a sigh. The house felt warm and inviting, as if welcoming me back. Everything was just as I'd left it. "How about you go and pick out a room? I'll find food."

Russell circled the living room, before settling on the wooden branch stuck in the corner.

"You can pick anywhere," I said to him. "It doesn't have to be there."

He ruffled his feathers, seeming content with his decision.

"It's your choice. There are plenty of spaces upstairs if you need privacy to do... crow stuff."

Hilda scuttled under the magic cabinet in the corner.

I ducked down and peered under it. There was a small pile of cotton in one corner, some carpeting, and a mural painted on one wall. "Is this your home, Hilda?"

171

She ran out and pressed a front leg against my hand. "I'm happy here. I've always lived under here. I've done it up how I like it. And I don't want much space because it'll only need cleaning. This'll do for me."

"I'm picking my own bedroom upstairs," Nugget said. "I need a place of silence and solitude."

"Won't you be lonely up there on your own?" Hilda said. "We'll all be down here."

"I like my own company." Nugget turned and sauntered out of the living room.

"He'll be back," Hilda said. "He likes to think he's his own cat, but he enjoys being with us as much as we like being with him."

"Sometimes, he's got a strange way of showing it," I said.

"Nugget's cautious about getting close to people. He adored Magda."

"I remember. He used to follow her everywhere. And when she sat down, he'd drape himself around her shoulders and fall asleep."

"He did. Nugget took it hard when things went wrong for Magda. And he's worried you'll leave us, too."

I held out my hand for Hilda to step into so we could carry on a conversation and then stood. "Staying here isn't safe long-term. I'm not saying I don't want to stay, but something happened to my stepmom in this house. She lost control of her magic. What if the same happens to me?"

"That's what everyone claims happened, but no one knows for certain," Hilda said. "We were all here, and none of us saw what was going on until it was too late."

"I don't remember much about that time. It's a blur. And it happened so fast. Everything was great. Then the darkness appeared, and it all went wrong. Then Magda got arrested. I never got to talk to her, to figure out what happened."

"You're a lot like her," Hilda said. "Even though you're not related by blood, you have the same stubborn streak. You get on a particular path and don't want to get off, even though it's taking you in a direction you don't like."

"I need to find a direction that'll keep me safe. I can't stay hidden here for long. The Magic Council will be hunting for me. They'll know I escaped from the cell by now."

"They won't come looking here. And if they do, all they'll see is a pile of rubble. This gives us time to find a solution."

I smiled. "It does. But since I'm staying, I want to deal with the spirit attached to Luna. I have to help her. She won't recover until I get rid of him."

Hilda bobbed up and down on my hand. "If you capture the spirit and set Luna free, will you leave us?"

I looked around the house. It called to me. I wanted to stay. "I'm thinking about staying."

"That's good enough for now. You think about it while you make our amazing food. Then we have work to do."

A few hours later, and after some major over-indulging of flies on Hilda's part, it was down to business.

173

I set Hilda on top of the magic cabinet and pulled it open. "Let's see what we've got that will get rid of this ghost once and for all."

Hilda scuttled into the cabinet and rooted through an open drawer.

I leafed through old spell books, checked the contents of dozens of jars and vials, and immersed myself in happy memories of my childhood.

I took out a clean spirit jar, salt, camphor, and a feather quill. "I'm thinking we go old school magic. Odessa's spirit trapping baskets sort of worked, so I don't want to change everything. If we create a spell to trap negative energy and contain it in this jar, it should suck the ghost inside."

Hilda ran up my arm. "And put a tiger opal in the bottom of the jar. The one with the most energy. Ghosts hate those."

I tested several stones until I found one vibrating with power. It went in the bottom of the jar. Then I added cinnamon, bay leaves, a sprinkle of dried arrow root, and a containment spell.

"You should stick with the tiger opals to make a wider containment field," Hilda said. "They're amazing at taking away negative energy. And it sounds like this ghost is full of negativity."

We gathered four more strong tiger opals.

I pulled opened the bottom drawer of the magic cabinet. There were a dozen small journals piled inside, and a box Magda used to store her favorite necklaces.

I smiled as I took out a journal. She'd kept journals her whole life, and would often note down unusual events of the day, or simply record her feelings.

She'd encouraged me to journal, but I'd never gotten into it.

I flicked through the pages. It was full of spells and incantations with her comments on their effectiveness. She'd tried different healing spells, calming spells, and repair spells. All of it positive, useful magic. Nothing that hinted at the darkness that had consumed her.

"Less reading and more action," Hilda said. "We've got work to do."

I closed the journal and flipped open the box. The faint smell of jasmine drifted out, making my heart clench. The smell was Magda. She'd grown jasmine around the porch. I'd have to see if it was still alive and get it blooming again.

A purple lump of amethyst caught my eye. It was looped on a simple black string; the stone polished smooth.

"Indigo, we have a ghost to deal with." Hilda hopped off my knee and scurried away.

I grabbed a bag and placed the tiger opals and magic items inside. I also tied the amethyst around my neck and stuffed a journal inside the bag. It had taken hours to catch the ghost the last time I'd gone to Luna's apartment, so I may as well have reading material to keep me company.

"You're coming with me?" I said to Hilda as she returned and settled on my shoulder.

"Of course. We all are."

"Then you'd better go wake Nugget and hope he's not too grumpy. It's time to catch this spirit and get my best friend back." If I couldn't solve my own problems, I'd solve Luna's. She deserved it.

Chapter 16

We hurried out of the house, and I took a minute to check no one was around to see us leaving. Darkness was our cover as we headed to Luna's apartment to confront the spirit.

Russell soared over our heads as we continued along the road, heading past the quiet stores and houses. It was a chilly night, which worked in our favor. The cold would discourage most people from coming out and noticing us. Word would be all around the village that a dangerous Ash witch was on the loose and needed to be stopped, and I didn't want anyone attempting that. My days of hurting people were over.

Hilda rode on my shoulder as Nugget kept to the shadows as we hurried along, while Russell continued to fly overhead, acting as our lookout.

I was dressed head-to-toe in black, with a baseball cap on so if I did bump into anyone, I could avoid being recognized.

The ten-minute walk to the apartment seemed to take forever, and I jumped at any noise or animal hoot from the trees. If I got caught, I'd be in so much trouble.

Finally, we were standing outside Luna's apartment building. We hurried into the communal area and up the stairs, stopping when we reached the apartment door.

Nugget's fur puffed out all around him, making him look like a cute, cartoon cat. I was tempted to pet him, but resisted. I didn't need him to go into attack cat mode on me. One permission to tickle him didn't give me a free pass to ruffle his fur anytime I wanted.

"Are you sensing something you don't like?" I said.

"There's nothing good inside that apartment," he said.

"You don't have to come in," I said.

"We're all going in." Hilda was perched on my shoulder. "We're your backup. We'll help if you need it."

"And from the feel of this spirit, you'll need all the help you can get," Nugget said. "Are you sure you're up to the challenge?"

I nodded. I felt confident about using my magic on this ghost. He'd hurt someone I cared about and thrown me out of a window. The thing deserved to pay.

I pushed the door open and peeked inside. What looked like soot covered the floor, and there were black streaks along the wall as if the place had been damaged by fire.

"Russell, do a quick sweep to make sure there's nothing too nasty lurking in the shadows," I said.

He shot through the gap and flew into each room, returning a moment later.

"Anything bad to report?" I whispered.

177

He gave a whole body shudder and squawked.

"He's not happy, but he didn't see anything evil," Hilda said.

"You got all that from a single squawk?" I said.

"Yes. And his body language. We've been together a long time. We know each other's moods," Hilda said.

"Okay then. Let's go say hello to this ghost and ask him to leave." I patted the bag slung over my shoulder. It contained everything to drain and capture this ghost. Hopefully.

I left the front door open in case we needed to make a hasty escape and walked along the hallway. "Coo-eee! I'm back. Aren't you going to come out and offer me coffee and cake?"

"It's best not to aggravate the ghost," Hilda whispered.

"He already hates me. Nothing I do will change that." I tiptoed along the hallway. "Come out, come out, wherever you are. We need to have a few words."

The temperature dropped, and a dark mist swirled around me.

"Aaaww! There you are, looking all spooky and evil. I hoped the last time I caught you, you'd given up and moved on."

A low laugh rumbled through the air like menacing thunder.

I pulled out the tiger opals. "Russell, you know what to do. One in each corner of this room. We don't want our little ghostly friend getting away while we're having a chat."

Russell scooped up each opal in turn and set them in the four corners of the room. They'd act like a barrier to keep the ghost from escaping once I'd contained him.

"It's time you let Luna go," I said. "She's a good person. She doesn't need your attention. Leave this place."

"Make me, witch," a growly voice said. "This is my home. You're trespassing."

"And so are you. Luna lives here. Leave her alone."

"What makes you think you can save her?"

"I have to. She's my friend. She deserves better than to be messed with by you."

"That didn't answer my question. Why you? Luna's tried to get rid of me and failed. You've also tried once. Why come back when you know you'll lose?"

The dark mist around us intensified, making me shiver. But I wasn't being intimidated by a bully who wouldn't show himself. "Because I have my friends helping me this time."

"These poor excuses for familiars are your only friends? I don't know whether to laugh or feel sorry for you."

"Hey! We're great familiars, you big floaty mass of crud," Nugget said. "The best. We belong to an Ash witch. You don't get better than that."

The ghost cackled. "You've never belonged to an Ash witch. You were brought into the family by good fortune and an advantageous marriage. That doesn't make you important."

"How do you know that?" This ghost was bugging me. He knew too much about my life.

"I'm all powerful. I have knowledge that—"

"He can float through walls and likes to earwig on private matters." Nugget flicked his tail. "Let me give you some advice. No one likes an eavesdropper."

I snorted a laugh. "They may have been my stepmom's familiars, but they're mine now. I'm a full Ash witch. Therefore, they're important to me. They're also under my protection. Hurt them and I'm coming for you."

Russell flapped his wings from his position on the back of the couch, Hilda jigged on my shoulder, and Nugget stared up at me.

I glanced down at Nugget. "I mean it. All of you, if you want to be my familiars. No pressure, though."

Nugget looked like he was about to hack up a hairball. "I'll think about it."

"I'm happy to take on that position," Hilda said. "So is Russell."

I nodded. They were mine, even though I'd protested about having them in my life. I couldn't deny they were part of my life any longer. I also needed to stop denying I wanted familiars. It had been my childhood dream to have a cat familiar, but a crow and a hairy spider were also cool.

Russell gave an excited sounding caw, and Hilda did another little dance on my shoulder.

The ghost growled and spun around me, still nothing more than a cold mist in the room.

"Your show pony tricks are getting tired. It's time you left this place," I said. "Move on to a different journey."

"And if I choose to stay here?"

"Then you'll be captured. You'll have no freedom."

"No freedom. You'd know all about that. You had yours taken from you. Your magic was destroyed. I can sense your lack of power. You're no threat to me."

"I have plenty of power." I glanced at Nugget, and he nodded. "And I have my awesome backup. You can't fight us all."

"I can. And it won't be a challenge."

I pulled the ghost jar out of my bag, opened the lid and placed it on the floor in the center of the room.

A menacing growl echoed around me. "You will not contain me. I refuse to leave. Luna is mine."

"She belongs to no one. You'll let her go. This is your last warning. Release Luna, or you'll be captured and never feel freedom again."

A blast of cold rammed through me, making me stagger back. I fell against the wall, my teeth chattering. "Is everyone okay?"

"We're good." Nugget's fur was even puffier, Hilda clung to my shoulder, and Russell hovered in the air above my head.

"I guess that was your way of saying no," I said to the ghost.

"You'll fail, Ash witch, you always do. Your past is littered with failures and so is your future. You're a mistake. The Magic Council should never have let you go."

"I've made plenty of mistakes in my past, but at least I learned from them. And I'm still learning."

I looked at my familiars and pride made my chest swell. I wasn't scared of this ghost, not with them here. And Luna's safety mattered, and I wasn't giving up on her.

I waved my hands over the open container, evoking the containment spell.

"Your magic can't trap me," the ghost said.

Frost crackled against the glass as the temperature grew even colder.

Nugget, Russell, and Hilda moved into position, standing around the container and blasted their own magic into it, strengthening the spell.

"Leave!" the ghost yelled. "You're not welcome here."

"Neither are you. It's time to go. You won't go willingly, so you leave me no choice." I thrust out my hands and spread the containment spell around the room.

The mist swelled and pulsed, and I saw flashes of a dark image in it. It was a large, bulky shape that almost touched the ceiling.

I placed both hands over the container and evoked the containment spell again. The magic flowed effortlessly from my hands. It felt amazing to use magic properly again.

There was an angry wail, then the mist vanished, spiraling into the container.

"Quick! Close the lid," I said.

Nugget knocked the lid down with his head and stood on top.

I snapped it closed, then looked around the room and let out a sigh. It felt peaceful. There were no black marks on the walls, the soot had gone, and the temperature was returning to normal.

"We did it! We captured the ghost." I knelt and prodded the container with a finger. "That was easy."

"I never had any doubt we'd do it," Nugget said. "With us by your side, it was a simple job."

"Luna's going to be thrilled. She can get out of the hospital and come home." I risked petting Nugget on the head, while Hilda danced around the room with Russell, who bobbed along beside her.

I laughed as I watched them do a funny jig. I couldn't wait to see how Luna was doing. Now the ghost was trapped, he'd no longer have such a hold over her, and after he'd been contained for a while, he'd weaken so she could get free of his grip.

"We should celebrate," I said.

"Discreetly," Nugget said. "We don't want the Magic Council catching us feasting on doughnuts in celebration."

"You're right. And that's something else I need to deal with. The Magic Council will be furious I escaped. I have to convince them I did it for the right reasons. They wouldn't help Luna, so I had to. I wasn't using magic to do bad things."

Hilda hopped on my hand. "We'll stick up for you. And so will your friends. Once Luna recovers, the Magic Council will see you used your magic for good. You wouldn't have risked your life to capture this ghost if you weren't a good witch. That'll stand in your favor."

"It's worth a try arguing that point, but I need to get the Magic Council to listen to me. They've never been keen on doing that."

"We'll keep fighting until they see sense. They can't drain you of your magic now you're using it for good," Hilda said.

"We'll take the ghost to show them," Nugget said. "That's evidence you're doing good these days."

The container on the floor jumped a foot in the air.

I slammed my hand on it. "We need to figure out what to do about the Magic Council later. Let's get this container back to the house and secure it. We don't want—"

The lid blasted off, and a foul smelling gray mist shot out. I breathed some of it in and gagged. It stank like the carcass of a rotting animal that had been heated in the sun.

Russell squawked and flew out of the way of the mist. It pursued him, shooting around the room and lunging at him.

"Stay away from Russell!" I blasted out a fireball, not even thinking what I was doing, simply reacting to the ghost escaping. My magic worked perfectly. The fire blasted through the mist and it retreated, only to turn its attention to Nugget.

Before he had a chance to run away, the mist descended on him and he vanished from sight.

"No! Get away from my cat." I threw myself at the mist. I held another fireball in my hand, but didn't throw it in case it hit Nugget. I kept grabbing at the mist, trying to break through, but every handful simply slipped through my fingers.

Russell swooped down and plunged through the mist. He disappeared for a few seconds, before rolling out the other side and landing on his back. He hopped to his feet and shook his head.

"Is Nugget hurt? Did you see him?" I gasped out.

Russell gave a short, sharp squawk.

"He's in there. He's alive," Hilda said, from her position on my shoulder.

Nugget was suddenly ejected from the mist. He flopped onto his belly, gasping, his fur covered in green slime.

"No one hurts my familiars and gets away with it." I blasted a fireball straight into the mist.

It exploded, scattering around the room. The mist swiftly gathered by the doorway and tried to get through, but the power from the tiger opals stopped it.

I let out a sigh of relief. The ghost was contained to this room. That would make him easier to get back in the ghost jar, even if he was in this misty form.

The ghostly mist reared back and roared so loudly it made my ears hurt.

I stood tall, Hilda on my shoulder, Russell on the other, and Nugget standing beside me looking gooey but determined.

"We're not afraid of you. You won't beat us. Give up now."

Two glowing eyes appeared in the mist. There was a laugh, and the mist gathered into a large hulking beast. It shot toward me.

I thrust out my hands and blasted a knock back spell. The mist slowed, but kept on coming.

185

Nugget hissed and orange sparks of magic shot out of him as he pounced and slammed into the mist.

Russell took off from my shoulder and dive-bombed in and out of the mist.

Hilda stood on her back limbs and threw out a sparkling webbing that covered the mist and made it fizzle.

"Keep going, everyone," I said through gritted teeth as I shoved more power into my knock back spell. "We're wearing him down."

The ghostly mist was inching closer, but he had to tire soon. I needed him to. My magic was draining fast, but I was focusing so hard that I only felt mild surprise that my spells were having such an effect on this ghost.

The mist reared up, poured over my head and shot down toward me. An aching cold flooded down my throat, and I couldn't see.

"No!" I lost control of my spell and batted my hands through the mist, my insides turning to ice. As I dropped to the floor, Russell was alarm calling and Nugget was hissing and snarling, and then nothing.

Chapter 17

My head throbbed as I slowly blinked my eyes open. I tried to lift one arm, but didn't have the strength to move.

I slid my gaze to the window. Dawn was breaking outside. I'd been unconscious for hours. The last thing I remembered were the cries of anger and distress from Russell and Nugget. Then everything had gone black.

The foul smell of rotting carcass filled my nose. It was sweltering hot inside the apartment, and the black soot had reappeared on the floor.

I traced my fingers through the gritty substance and it made my skin sting.

I had to get up. The others could be injured. They could be dead. I'd been out of it for such a long time, anything could have happened.

I sucked in a steadying breath, only just managing not to gag as I got another whiff of the stench in the room. I rolled onto my side, and then onto my hands and knees, feeling like I'd gone ten rounds with a prize fighter. Sweat dripped off me.

It felt like I'd been thrown into the depths of hell. If I didn't recognize Luna's apartment, I'd think that was exactly where I'd been taken.

A shuffling noise hit my ears, and I tensed. Was it the ghost returning to finish me off? I let out a gurgle of relief as Hilda appeared from under a pile of soot.

A lump lodged in my throat. She was missing two legs. "Hilda!" I gasped out. "What happened?"

She hobbled over, before collapsing on top of my hand and wheezing out a breath. "The ghost attacked us all. I've never felt anything like it."

"Where are the others?"

"Russell was tossed out the window. I didn't see what happened to Nugget. He fought so hard. He was still fighting when you lost consciousness."

I struggled up onto my knees, and the world tipped. I blinked slowly several times to dislodge the wave of dizziness, but it only helped a fraction. I crawled to the window ledge and hauled myself up.

The lump in my throat grew bigger as I saw Russell on the ground. One wing was bent at a horribly unnatural angle.

Hilda crawled up to join me and leaned against my cheek. "I'll go down and see to him. You look around for Nugget."

"Are you sure you're up to it? You must be in pain."

"I can still get around if I'm careful. I'll use my webbing to get me to the ground floor."

"What happened to the ghost?" I glanced around to see the tiger opals had shattered and the ghost jar was in pieces.

188

"He disappeared after the attack. I'm sure he'll be back, so we don't have much time." Hilda crawled away and abseiled down the side of the building.

There was no way I was waiting around here for the ghost to come back. My head throbbed, my magic was drained, and my familiars were hurt. I gathered what was left of my strength and stood on wobbly knees.

"Nugget, are you in here?" I hunted around the room, sliding my hand through piles of stinging soot to see if he'd been buried beneath one, but he wasn't in the living room.

I checked the bathroom and then the bedroom. There was still no sign of Nugget, and the apartment was getting hotter by the second.

I staggered into the kitchen and froze. Nugget was flat out on one of the worktops. He wasn't moving. I raced over and rested my hand on his chest. There were no signs of life. I flipped him over and pressed my hand against his chest, conjuring the strongest healing spell I knew.

I yelped as I was blasted back and slammed into the wall, collapsing into a heap on the floor. The skin on my palm was burned from using the spell.

A sob of despair threatened to come out, but I pressed my lips together. I had to fix this. I wouldn't accept I'd lost my familiar.

I pulled myself up, using the wall to balance, and wobbled back to Nugget. "Wake up! You can't be dead. You've lived for over forty years. Don't let this mission kill you." I pressed my hand on his chest and tried the healing spell again. This time, a trickle of ineffective magic came out. It danced over his skin

189

for a few seconds, before fading. It was pathetic. I was pathetic. My magic was broken.

I tried different healing spells, and they all misfired. I couldn't do magic any more. Whatever that ghost had done to me, I was too damaged to be repaired.

I dropped my head onto Nugget's still stomach as tears dripped down my cheeks and landed in his fur. This place was no haven for witches. Ever since I'd come back, there'd been trouble. I should never have come home. My familiars were injured or dead, Luna's life was at risk because I couldn't contain the spirit attacking her, and when word got back to the Magic Council that I was on the loose and using illegal magic, they'd grab me and turn me into a shadow.

I should have stayed where I was. I was better off alone. And everyone else was safer if I stayed out of their way.

I didn't want to give up on Nugget. There was no way I'd have his death on my conscience. I swiped the tears from my cheeks and placed both hands flat on his stomach. He would wake up. I ignored the throbbing pain from my own injuries and pushed everything I had into healing him.

For a few seconds, magic ran through me and pulsed into Nugget, but the healing spell wouldn't stay contained. It scattered off my skin, around the worktop, and then slammed into the ceiling, sending plaster raining down on us.

I covered Nugget so he wouldn't be injured and waited for the magic to fade.

Nothing I could do would bring him back. I was only hurting myself and messing up this apartment by trying.

"I'm so sorry, Nugget. I never meant for this to happen." I tickled him between the ears in the spot he liked. Of course, he didn't respond.

I stepped back and took in the chaos. Luna's apartment was almost destroyed, with holes in the walls and mold covering the ceiling. And from the growing feeling of malevolence, the ghost was coming back, most likely to finish what he started.

What should I do? It was best for everyone if I walked away from this. If I did, I'd be leaving behind a huge mess I'd caused. But if I stayed, I had no idea how to fix things. I'd tried to capture this ghost and failed. I'd injured my familiar, and I'd have plenty to answer for when the Magic Council finally caught up with me. And they would. I was living on borrowed time.

I grabbed a tea towel and placed it over Nugget. Then headed back to the window Hilda had climbed out of and looked out, relieved to see Russell was upright and holding one wing out as Hilda talked to him.

I gathered up the remains of the magic equipment I'd brought with me and went back to the kitchen. I carefully picked up Nugget and tucked him inside the bag. With a last look around the destroyed apartment, I walked away and shut the door.

I stumbled down the stairs, out the main doors, and over to Hilda and Russell.

I knelt in front of him. "How are you doing? It looks like a wing got broken."

He made a sad sounding squawk.

"It is broken." Hilda perched herself on my hand.

"I'd offer to heal you both, but my healing magic doesn't seem to be working. I tried several spells in the apartment and they backfired." I showed them my singed palm.

"We can heal ourselves, providing we get back to the house," Hilda said. "Who were you trying to heal?"

I rested a hand against Nugget. I couldn't tell them he was gone. They were a team, and I'd just lost their friend. "I hurt my ankle and was trying to heal myself."

"Come back to the house. There are healing tonics there. Have a few of those and you'll feel better," Hilda said.

I shook my head. I couldn't be around them any longer. I'd caused too much damage. "You two go ahead. I'll stay here with Nugget and make sure everything is okay."

"Do you think the ghost is still inside?" Hilda said. "We can stay and help if you think he'll cause more problems."

"He's definitely lurking, but seems satisfied with the destruction he's caused for now."

"It's no wonder Luna feels so terrible, with this being attached to her," Hilda said. "He's filled with darkness. We'll find a way to defeat him. He just got the better of us this time."

I nodded, not wanting to reveal my true fears about this ghost. There was no way I could defeat him. I wasn't a strong enough witch. "You both go back to the house and get yourselves fixed up."

"Are you sure you don't want us to stay?" Hilda said. "We can keep an eye out to see if the ghost comes back."

"You go. I won't be long." With a heavy heart, I watched Hilda and Russell leave. Hilda had a strange tilting walk because of her lost limbs, and Russell held out his damaged wing, making him lean to the right as he hobbled along.

I made the short walk to the cemetery at the edge of Witch Haven. I lifted Nugget out of my bag and held him close.

"Let's find somewhere nice for you to go." There was a specific part of the cemetery set aside for familiars. Nearly every witch had a familiar, and cherished them like they were her children, and they were always given a respectful send-off.

I couldn't offer that to Nugget, but I could find him a decent final resting place.

"This tree looks good. It's shady, so you won't get too hot. And most of these nearby graves are also cat familiars. You may make new friends." I choked on my words.

I set Nugget down and hunted out the equipment store. I broke the lock, found a large shovel, and returned to the tree, where I dug a deep hole nearby. The ground was easy going because it was soft, and I soon had a space big enough for Nugget.

I took off my jacket, put him in it, and placed him in the hole. "I let you down. You were a great familiar. You taught me so much when I was growing up. It shouldn't have ended this way." I kissed him on the head, tucked my jacket around him carefully so he was snug, and covered him over with the soft, damp earth.

I made a makeshift headstone from a pile of small stones, so I wouldn't forget the location of his grave. I'd figure out a permanent headstone for him as soon as I could.

And once I was brave enough to let Hilda and Russell know what happened to Nugget, I'd ask them to sort it out. They'd know what kind of thing he'd like.

I returned the shovel to the equipment store and then wiped mud off my hands.

This was a darkly fitting way to end my visit to Witch Haven. The last time I'd been here, people had died, and now it had happened all over again. It was the proof I needed that returning was a wrong move.

I closed my eyes as I stood over Nugget's grave and said a silent farewell.

It was time to go and never return.

Chapter 18

I rolled over and stared at the beige wall. It had been this color when I'd moved into my tiny apartment in York Town. I kept thinking I'd spruce the place up, make it homelier, but I could never gather the enthusiasm to make any changes.

I closed my eyes and tried to force myself back to sleep, but the opportunity to escape from my grim reality with more slumber had passed.

It had been five days since I'd walked out of Witch Haven. Five days since the ghost had beaten me and Nugget had died.

I dreamt about him every night. I'd wake up and think my visit home had been a dream, or Nugget was still alive and would be sitting on the end of the bed being rude to me and telling me where I could pet him.

But he was gone. I hadn't saved him. And I'd failed to save Luna. I'd even been too much of a coward to tell anyone I was going. I'd just walked away.

It didn't matter, not anymore. Life was back to normal. I should never have thought I could have familiars, make new friends, and resurrect old friendships. When I'd gotten the demands from the

Magic Council, I should have ignored them. If I had, no one would have been hurt or died.

After another fifteen minutes of convincing myself, I should stay in bed, my stomach grumbled. I rolled out of my messy sheets, stuffed my feet into my slippers, and wandered into the tiny kitchenette. There were only three rooms in this apartment. The bedroom, the open plan living room and kitchen, and the bathroom. It had everything I needed, plus it was cheap, and on an estate where everyone minded their business. I could come and go as I pleased, and no one asked me what I was doing, or who I was. I didn't even know my neighbor's names.

Was it safe to come back here? Most likely not. Every day, I expected someone from the Magic Council to barge in and arrest me. But no one showed up. Maybe they were grateful I'd left Witch Haven. If I was out of their way, I couldn't do the place any more harm.

I made an instant coffee and stood by the window, looking out at the next apartment block's gray wall as I sipped it.

This life would do. I should have known better than to go back to my past. I should have ignored Luna's requests for assistance with that ghost. Now, I was free from all that. I could try something new.

I looked around the apartment again. I would repaint these walls. It would give me something to do and take my mind off the mess I'd left behind. Or I could travel. I could go somewhere where no one knew me and they had no idea about my past. There were places magic users lived because they didn't like using their abilities. They preferred to blend in with everyone else and pretend they were normal. I could do that. And since my magic was misfiring, there was no point in using it.

My hand was still painful from my healing spells backfiring when I'd failed to save Nugget.

I was so broken as a witch that I shouldn't even bother trying to be one. I could go visit one of these communes where magic wasn't used. I'd fit in there. It could work.

I sighed and sipped more of my bitter coffee. I hadn't heard a single sound since I'd gotten up. This place was gravely quiet. People tended to go out late at night, coming back at dawn. I didn't dwell on what they were doing during those dark hours. Maybe they just worked the night shift. Maybe not.

I used to like the quiet. It meant there was little chance of being bothered. But after spending time with Russell, Hilda, and Nugget, the silence felt like it was pressing in on me.

I shook my head. I'd been in Witch Haven for less than a week. Nothing was different about my life. It couldn't have changed me in that short amount of time. All I'd done was go in, cause chaos, and then leave.

I rested my head against the smeared window.

Things had changed. I wanted my familiars back. They felt like they were mine and I was responsible for them.

Not only that, I'd killed one of them. Nugget had only been in Luna's apartment because of my crazy plan to save her and be the hero. It was a vanity thing. I was saving Luna because it was a massage to my damaged reputation. I'd hoped that stepping up and being the good witch would give the Magic Council pause before they stripped me of my power. I was a terrible best friend. I was a fraud.

And this was what happened. One familiar dead, two injured, my best friend dying, and the Magic Council intent on destroying my ability.

But there was no place for me in Witch Haven. This was what I'd chosen. I liked the quiet, simple life, with no commitments. It made everything easier.

I finished my coffee and made another. I had no food in the cupboard, but couldn't be bothered to go out and re-stock. Coffee would do. Maybe I'd order a takeout later. That would be fun.

I looked around the room. I could go get paint samples. Maybe paint this place purple. That would add some vibrancy to its soulless atmosphere.

I grimaced and wiped a cobweb out of the corner of the window. When had my life gotten so dull? If takeout and painting walls were the highlight of my existence, was there even much point in carrying on? Everything I touched got tainted, and that wasn't fair to the people who got messed with.

I settled into the faded armchair by the window and pulled out Magda's journal. I'd been reading a couple of pages every day since I'd come back. I could never get very far into it, because reading her notes and ideas about magic made me angry and want to thump something. We'd had a great life, and she'd stuffed it up.

Ash witches had once been respected and kicked serious butt when it came to evildoers. We were known for upholding magic rules. Even the Magic Council had respected the Ash witch coven and often come to my ancestors for guidance.

"What went wrong?" I whispered. I turned a page and discovered a dried piece of lavender.

I pulled it out and smelled it as I continued to flick through the pages, slowing when the writing became erratic.

My stomach tightened and horror trickled through my veins like acid. The spells written on the pages grew darker, and alongside them, the unstable thoughts of my stepmom were clear.

She detailed feeling paranoid and unsafe and needing to find strong magic to protect herself. I had no idea what she needed to be protected from.

There were several pages that had been raked through hard with a pen, no words, just scrawling ink, suggesting anger and rage had been poured onto the pages.

I flicked through until I discovered several blank pages. I continued flicking, and then the writing began again.

Turning back to the blank pages, I pressed my hand against one. My heart skipped a beat. There was magic on this page.

I set my coffee down and cracked my fingers. My magic still wasn't functioning properly, and if I tried a spell on this book, I could set it on fire. But there was something hidden on this page, and I wanted to know what it was.

"Okay, let's see what you're hiding." I had nothing left to lose. If I set fire to the book, it would be more evidence that magic was no longer for me.

I evoked a reveal spell on the page and held my breath.

At first, nothing happened. The magic trickled out of my hand in a slow, painful wave. Magic shouldn't feel like that. The energy felt forced and fractured.

My breath hitched as faint marks appeared on the page. There was something there. Since the book hadn't exploded into a fireball, I risked using the reveal spell again.

This time, words appeared.

My gut tightened, and my eyes widened as I read the first line.

Indigo, if you're reading this, then I'm dead...

I swallowed and licked my lips. Magda had hidden these words for me to find.

The surprise at discovering this hidden message had tears springing to my eyes. I blinked them away. I had to know more.

It's too late for me. What's been set in motion can't be stopped. I wish with every bone in my body that I could have prevented this tragedy. But I had to protect you. My world revolved around you, and when your life was threatened, I had to act.

I scrunched my brow. I don't remember being threatened. What was she talking about?

I was contacted by a dark witch. She threatened your life if I didn't follow her orders.

"You should have kicked her butt," I muttered. Magda may not have been an Ash witch, but she'd had an awesome set of magic skills.

At first, I ignored her demands. The coven she was a part of wanted to take over Witch

200

Haven. They had plans to turn it into a place for wickedness. I refused, but then they showed me they'd harvested your personal items. They had your hair, blood, and clothing. They threatened to kill you if I didn't do their bidding.

I loved you like you were my child. I couldn't have any of my own, and when I married your father, I was so happy to join the family. I must admit, I was intimidated by your power. You had so much and it shone brightly. I was honored you considered me a member of your coven. I hoped I'd never let you down. And at the time I'm writing these words, I know I haven't, but I soon will. And you will be ashamed to have known me.

I didn't even realize I was crying until a tear dripped onto the journal. I quickly dabbed it off and kept reading.

I tried to bargain with this witch, but it was a choice of your life or sacrificing other magic users' free will to her. She wants them under her control so she can have an army of powerful magic users to do her work.

I can't lose you. Your father was taken from us far too young, and it would destroy me if you were taken too. I'll do whatever I have to so you remain safe.

Even if it means harming others.

Guilt squeezed tight around my heart. All those people had died so I could live? It felt wrong. I wasn't worth all those innocent lives.

Although this witch has a dark soul, I believe her when she says no lives will be lost. Providing I cast the magic she demands over the village, you'll

201

be spared. But it's dangerous magic, and unstable. I've been practicing for weeks to gain control of it, but I fear I'm losing myself. It's the darkest magic I've ever experienced. It constantly breaks its boundaries and goes off in directions I don't anticipate. I'm sure you've noticed my behavior has changed.

I'm trying to keep you safe, but I fear I'm not strong enough.

I swiped away more tears. "You shouldn't have believed that witch. Dark magic can never be trusted." I turned the page to find more text.

Magda's usually neat handwriting grew more erratic. Perhaps she feared she'd be caught recording this information and had to scribble quickly.

There's little time left. I'm casting the magic tonight. I'm so sorry you've become involved. I never meant for you to be exposed to this magic I must use, but it refused to stay contained. I deeply regret you were touched by these dark spells. It's not your fault. You are strong. You will survive this.

Our time is short. The dark witch comes tonight. When she arrives, she'll expect to see Witch Haven under her control. All 666 residents will be hers. Less two.

I'm taking you and the familiars out of the village. I'll cast the magic and then we'll leave before it affects us. I won't be a slave to this witch's evilness. I'm sorry other people will be harmed by what I'm about to do, but I cannot lose you. You mean more to me than anything.

Once I've done what this witch commands, she's promised to return your personal items to me. I've arranged a drop-off location so I can retrieve them before we leave the village. You'll be free of her darkness, and we can start a new life somewhere else.

I hope I can forgive myself for what I'm about to do.

Stay strong. You're an incredible witch. You have more power than you realize. I wish with all my heart you weren't involved, but it's too late to change anything. We'll soon be free from this nightmare, and our magic will heal us.

And once we are free from danger, we'll find a way to return Witch Haven to a safe, beautiful sanctuary for all.

Stay strong, daughter. And remember, I'll always be there for you. No matter what you need, no matter what kind of trouble you get yourself in, I will be here.

She signed off with two kisses.

I drew in a ragged breath. Magda hadn't been bad. She'd never meant to kill anyone. She'd been tricked. All this time, I'd had no idea.

The back of my hand came away damp after I'd swiped it across my cheek. I had to make sure her name was cleared and her reputation restored. Here was proof that no one was supposed to die that fateful day.

I couldn't agree with what she'd done, choosing to save me and risk so many other people, but I understood. She'd been so protective of me, always promising to keep me safe. And Magda had been a strong witch, so must have figured she could control whatever dark magic she'd been forced into using.

My hand pressed against the page with her words on. I had to make this right. The truth about what happened to Magda must not be hidden. If residents in the village knew the truth, they may forgive her.

But I couldn't do this on my own. I had to go back to Witch Haven, and I needed my familiars by my side. I'd find the evil witch who'd done this and make her pay. She'd regret ever tangling with me and my family.

I clutched the journal to my chest. I'd been on my own for such a long time that it felt alien to need help, but it wasn't a weakness to admit you needed support.

And I'd doubted my own magic ability for too long. I'd always figured there was something broken inside me, something that made me turn to dark magic and destroy so many innocent lives.

None of it was my fault. Magda had been trying to protect me, but it had gone wrong, and I'd ended up involved in something dark that she'd tried to keep me away from.

I had to believe in my own magic. I used to be a powerful witch no one messed with. It was time I returned to that.

And to do that, I needed to go back to Witch Haven, protect my friends, and clear my family's name.

I just had to hope that when I returned, I'd be forgiven. There were a lot of people I needed to say sorry to.

I stood and walked to the apartment door. I should have faced my fears earlier. If I had, Nugget may still be alive. It was too late for him, but I'd give him an awesome send-off when I returned and make sure he had an incredible memorial.

I tossed a few things into a bag, placed Magda's journal inside, and left my apartment.

It was time to go home. And this time, I was staying.

Chapter 19

I waited until darkness fell before re-entering Witch Haven. This time, it felt natural to be back. I belonged here, and it was time people got used to that.

I kept to the back alleys and side streets, to avoid residents or members of the Magic Council noticing me, ducking into shadows if anyone came too close.

This was my chance to make things right, before the Magic Council caught up with me. I was prepared to face them. And this time, I wouldn't go quietly. Now I knew the truth about what happened to Magda, I needed to convince them a darkness had tried to infect Witch Haven, and it had nothing to do with either of us.

I patted my bag, reassured by the feel of the journal inside. It wasn't perfect proof, but it should be enough to give them pause. They'd reopen the investigation into what happened that day once they read the contents of this journal. And while they were looking into what really happened, I had to find a way to convince them not to take away my powers. Because I wanted revenge on this dark witch, and to do that, I needed to be in top magical fighting form.

Once the coast was clear, I headed to the house. I pressed my hands against the magic barrier concealing it from view, and it melted away. The reveal spell came easily, and I'd even healed my burns. It had never felt this effortless to use magic before.

All this time, had I been the problem? I was so full of doubt over my magic that I'd literally stopped it from working.

I headed to the front porch and up the steps. I opened the door and walked inside. I heard Russell's alarm call before I saw him.

He ran out from the living room, pecking at my feet and legs, one wing still held out at an awkward angle.

"Stop! There's no need to attack. It's me." I hopped back as his large wing smacked against my calf.

Russell squawked again and continued to flap at me.

"I understand you're angry, but I've come back. I'm sorry for what happened." I stumbled into the living room and tripped over something, landing heavily on my knees.

Russell bounced onto my back and hopped up and down, his talons sinking through my clothing and scratching me.

Something soft brushed across the back of my hand. I opened one eye to see Hilda staring up at me. "Hey! Any chance you can call off Russell's attack? He's not listening to me."

"No. What are you doing here?" Her black beady eyes were fixed on me as she rubbed her fangs together.

I huffed out a breath. I deserved the cold shoulder, the sharp looks, and talon attack. "I'm sorry. After everything that happened in the apartment, I thought the best thing to do was leave. That was wrong."

"It was. You didn't even say goodbye," Hilda said. "We were worried something bad had happened to you. We thought the Magic Council had arrested you again. Then Russell suggested the ghost had taken you. You scared us."

Russell squawked and jumped up and down.

"I know. I'm an idiot. I should never have done that. I got scared. I figured Witch Haven was better without me living here." I caught hold of Russell and eased his talons out of my hair. "I promise; I'll never leave again. I get how angry you are. You have every right to stamp and peck and squawk."

Russell squirmed out of my grip and hopped away to stand beside Hilda.

"Did you take Nugget with you when you left?" she said. "We've looked everywhere for him, but he's missing."

"Oh! Nugget." If they didn't already hate me, they would now. "He... um... he didn't make it. He fought the ghost, and... it killed him."

"That's impossible," Hilda said.

"I tried to revive him with a spell, but my magic misfired." I looked at my hands. "At least, I thought it did."

"No, you don't understand. Nugget can't die," Hilda said.

I gave her head a little pat, hoping it would give her comfort. "I know he was a tough old cat, but he wasn't breathing when I found him. I don't know what the ghost did, but—"

"No! Nugget has nine lives. Actually, he has way more than nine lives. You do know how old he is, don't you?"

A weird gurgling sound came out of my mouth. "You're saying he can die and come back to life?"

Hilda tap danced on the back of my hand. "Exactly that. Magda never wanted to lose him, so used magic to make sure he lived as long as she did. We were worried when she died in case the magic faded, but he kept on living. Although he has become much more cantankerous. I blame that on a side effect of being given eternal life. Or a ridiculously long life. We're still figuring that out."

I leaped up, taking Hilda with me. "Oh, crud! That means I've done something terrible to Nugget."

"What did you do?" Hilda said. "Where is he?"

"I didn't know. I thought he was dead. I couldn't leave his body in the apartment for the ghost to mess with, so... oh, heck! I buried him in the pet cemetery."

Russell squawked and flapped his one undamaged wing.

Hilda danced from side to side on my hand. "Oh! You're in so much trouble. He won't be happy. We'd better go dig him up."

Russell hopped to the open door.

209

"Wait, before we do that, let me heal you both. It's my small way of saying sorry." It would also give me time to figure out how to apologize to Nugget. I couldn't believe I'd buried him alive. Well, he was technically dead when I buried him, but I didn't know he'd regenerate.

Hilda backed away to the tips of my fingers. "Are you sure your magic is working well enough to do that? Healing spells take it out of you, and I'm missing two legs. You don't grow those back with an easy chant and a sprinkle of something simple."

"Positive. My magical malfunction was all up here." I tapped the side of my head. "Let me help you. Russell, you must be in a lot of pain with a broken wing."

He cawed mournfully and hopped closer.

I kneeled in front of him, placed Hilda on the floor, then rested my hands gently on either side of his damaged wing. I inhaled and blew out slowly, pulsing warm, healing magic through his broken bones, and imagining the wing strong, healed, and healthy.

After a minute, he cawed softly, stepped back and flapped both wings. He held them out, stretching his wings wide.

"You look so handsome." I grinned and clapped my hands.

Russell shot in the air and circled around us. I was getting used to his different tones, and the noise he made suggested joy.

"Now you, Hilda." I held out my hand.

She climbed into it again. "Are you sure about this?"

"Yes! Look at Russell. Don't you want your legs back?"

"More than anything."

"Then let's get you back to the eight-legged beauty you once were."

Regeneration spells were harder than general healing magic. If you lost focus for a second, the wrong body part could grow back, and there was no way I was messing this up for Hilda. She'd been my biggest supporter since I'd come back to Witch Haven.

I grounded myself, sensing the calm, welcoming warmth of my home. Hilda's warm little torso nestled on my palm, and I took a moment to focus on her whole body, sensing every hair on her remaining limbs and the slight shiver of her fangs. I imagined her whole and healthy, doing one of her jigs when she was excited.

A hot blast of magic emerged from my hand and encased her in a red glow. Hilda was my only focus as I pulsed the regeneration magic through her.

Her new limbs sprouted and uncurled to reveal two new, healthy legs.

I gently eased back my magic, drawing it inside me. "How do they feel?" I asked.

She jigged on my hand. "I feel ten years younger."

I scooped her up and placed her on my shoulder, before holding out my arm to Russell. "I hope you can forgive me. I promise, I'll make it up to you. No matter how long it takes. I can't keep running away from my problems. It solves nothing and only ends up hurting the people I care about."

211

Russell hopped onto my arm and then bobbed up to my other shoulder. He nudged me with his head.

Hilda tapped my cheek. "You're learning how to be a great witch again. But isn't there somewhere we need to be?"

"Of course! Let's go dig up Nugget, and hope he doesn't have too many murderous intentions toward me." I ducked out into the night again, speed walking to the cemetery.

"Russell, take to the wing and let us know if there's anyone to avoid," Hilda said.

He zoomed into the air, seeming happy he now had two functioning wings again.

"I can't believe I didn't think about magic being involved with Nugget's long life. He's so old," I said.

"Don't say that when you're within earshot of Nugget. He's sensitive about his advanced years," Hilda said. "But almost anything is possible when you have enough power."

I nodded. I really was out of practice when it came to magic. I kept believing what I was seeing, and that never worked when it came to the supernatural.

I raced into the cemetery and over to the pet burial area. As I arrived at the grave where I'd placed Nugget, something was wrong. The pile of stones I'd made as a temporary headstone had been scattered everywhere, and the earth was disturbed.

"Did someone dig him up?" I swallowed. "Or has he come back as a zombie cat?" A zombie Nugget would be a nightmare.

"I don't think he's been dug up by anyone. He must have dug himself out," Hilda said.

I grimaced and closed my eyes for a second. "He's going to be so mad at me, isn't he?"

"He is. He's plotting a nasty end for you."

I jumped as Nugget's voice carried down from the trees.

"What were you doing burying me in the ground? Have you lost your senses?"

I looked up into the trees where Nugget's voice came from. He was perched on a low branch, his fur covered in mud and his tail swishing back and forth.

Air whooshed out of me. "You're alive!"

"Top marks for observation. You didn't think you could get rid of me that easily, did you?"

"I had no idea you couldn't die. Hilda just told me. If I'd have known, I'd have never put you in the ground. I'm so sorry." I hurried to the base of the tree.

"You will be," he hissed at me.

I winced at the sharp tone. "You did do an excellent impression of being dead. You had me convinced."

"And I was dead for about half an hour. Magda's magic takes its sweet time to bring me back. Each time I die, I stay dead a little longer. I don't know why it works like that."

"That doesn't sound fun. Where do you go?" I said.

"Nowhere pleasant. But it's better than waking and finding myself covered in filth with your unwashed jacket tucked around me."

"Hey! That was my favorite jacket."

"You can have it back if you want to dig it up."

213

I glanced at the grave. "No, you're good."

Nugget sniffed. "I demand compensation for this assault."

He wasn't going to let this go. I didn't blame him. I'd be hugely cheesed off too if someone buried me before I had a chance to regenerate. "You'll get it. Whatever you need. But we have bigger things to worry about."

"Bigger than the fact you tossed me into the ground like a piece of garbage?"

"Nugget! I honestly thought the ghost had killed you. When I woke up, you were flat out on the kitchen worktop."

"You didn't even try to bring me back to life?"

"I tried, but my magic refused to work. But it's different now. I'm different, and I'm going to make that ghost pay, and then I'm going to make sure Luna is safe."

"You didn't do so well the last time you attempted that," Nugget said.

"Because I didn't believe in my abilities, and I didn't trust anyone I worked with. But I need all of you to make this work. I need my familiars' support and strength."

"Maybe we don't want to be your familiars," Nugget said.

A coldness clung to my heart. "I... I'd understand if you didn't want me."

"So you should. You're flaky, you run off at the first sign of trouble, and you treat your familiars like disposable assets. As I discovered to my cost." He flicked a piece of mud off his paw.

I hung my head. I had baulked at the first sign of trouble.

"We should give Indigo a second chance," Hilda said. "It must have been hard coming back here, given everything that happened."

Russell squawked loudly as he settled on my shoulder.

"Thanks, you two. It wasn't easy, but I'm glad I came back. I hadn't thought about this place for a long time. I figured I had no happy memories here, but that's not true. They came flooding back when I saw the house and met you all. Now, I want to stay if you'll have me."

"We don't want you, and neither does the Magic Council," Nugget said.

"Nugget! That's not nice," Hilda said.

"You try being nice when all you can taste is dirt."

"I'll get you fresh salmon. Would you like that?" I said.

Nugget sniffed. "It's a small start."

"And you're right. If I'm staying, I need to figure out how to get the Magic Council on my side. I'll make sure it happens. They aren't chasing me out of my home. Not again."

"They've been looking for you," Nugget said. "They came through here just after I dug myself out. They're not happy with you."

"I'm not happy with me either." I held my hands out to Nugget. "Need a hand getting down?"

He thrashed his tail at me. "I'm still angry with you."

I lowered my hands. "How about I tell you what I found in Magda's journal? It'll make your day. It's proof about her innocence."

"I'm listening," Nugget said. "But this better not be a ruse to get me back on side."

"It's not." I looked at Hilda and Russell, and they nodded. "The day Magda went rogue, it wasn't her fault. Another witch forced her to do it. She threatened my life and said if Magda didn't help, I'd be killed."

Hilda jigged on my shoulder. "I knew it! There had to be a reason she attacked the village."

"Magda hid the truth in the pages of her journal. Magic revealed it to me. And she never meant to get me involved, but the magic was too strong and I got infected."

Nugget inched closer along the branch. "That won't be enough to convince the Magic Council you're a trustworthy witch. It'll take more than that."

"It's something. I can show it to them. And if I make enough noise, they'll have to listen to me and reopen the investigation. There could be a dark witch coven still wanting to take over Witch Haven. They'll want to stop that."

"Good luck with that," Nugget said. "The second they find you, you'll be in prison."

I sighed, his dejection hurting. "Not if you all help me."

"I still want to be your familiar," Hilda said. "So does Russell."

Russell gave my ear a gentle nip.

"What about you, Nugget?" I said. "I'll understand if you want me to go, but I really hope you don't."

He jumped down from the tree and sauntered over. "I have a long list of demands. They must all be met before I finalize my decision on my future."

I grinned. "Whatever you say. But not now. We need to catch that ghost, save Luna, and then get Magda's name cleared."

Nugget twitched his nose. "That's acceptable. And it'll give me time to decide what I want as compensation."

"Nugget!" Hilda's tone was stern. "Indigo is our witch. We don't make demands on her."

"You can," I said. "And you should. I've been a terrible witch."

"You're a witch who lost her way, but now you're on the right road." Hilda jigged on my shoulder. "It's so good to be back together."

Russell cawed loudly in agreement.

"So, what's the plan to stop this ghost?" Hilda said.

"We gather strong enough magic to defeat him. Let's head back to the house and assemble the most powerful spells and potions we have."

"Are you sure you can handle that kind of magic?" Nugget said.

"Indigo fixed Russell's wing and regrew my missing limbs," Hilda said. "She can do this."

"My magic isn't misfiring anymore. I'm ready to go and kick evil spirit backside," I said.

We dashed back to the house. I couldn't stop smiling now I had my familiars back. Well, Nugget was still on the fence, but I'd convince him this was the best household to be a part of.

Half an hour of sorting through spells, potions, and ghost jars, and we were back at Luna's apartment, and heading up the stairs. It was time to get rid of this ghost once and for all.

The door wasn't locked when I tried the handle, and I eased it open and headed along the hallway. Everything seemed quiet, but I'd been fooled by this ghost before.

"Let's move," I whispered to the others. "Get the wards in place."

We worked our way around the apartment, laying out the magic to contain the ghost. We were using a containment spell to keep him in one room, enchanted gems to drain his power, and dream catchers containing positive energy, to cleanse the room of his negativity.

The skin on the back of my neck tingled. I was being watched. It had to be the ghost waiting to make his move.

"Don't tell me you're too scared to come out and play?" I stood in the center of the living room where the last attack had gone down. Hilda sat on my shoulder, Russell hovered in the air, and Nugget sat beside me, his eyes narrowed.

"It's not working," Nugget said.

"Give the magic a chance. This is the only room not containing any repelling magic. Wherever the ghost goes, he won't feel welcome, so he'll have no choice but to come this way and join the party," I said.

"And then we'll get him," Hilda said. "I believe in you, Indigo."

"You also believe in unicorns," Nugget muttered.

"They're real," Hilda said. "I've seen one."

Russell squawked an agreement.

Something slammed against a wall in another room, making me jump. "We've got his attention," I said.

"And he's not happy," Nugget said.

"We're stopping his fun. Whatever twisty reason this ghost has for attaching himself to Luna, it's coming to an end."

"Don't be so sure about that." The low, menacing voice of the ghost sounded in my right ear.

I spun around and backed away, sparking magic on my fingers. "Welcome to your new prison."

"This isn't a prison. This is my home. I choose to be here."

"Not anymore. You're trapped in this room. Now, it's time to leave." I produced a triple spelled ghost jar from my bag and held it out.

He growled, and the air in front of me shimmered as if the spirit was about to manifest.

"Show yourself. I'm not afraid of you."

"Then you're stupid."

"I'll admit, I was never top of the class, but I know what I'm doing. You can come quietly or you can fight me all the way. I don't care. But you are leaving this place."

Jagged flickers of black energy sparked around the room. "You failed to catch me the last time. I expect you were surprised to find the wrong spirit trapped in your pathetic basket."

"You know about that?"

"I know about everything. I encouraged the ghost into that trap. And I've followed your journey with interest since you returned to Witch Haven."

I tilted my head. "Why the interest in me?"

"Darkness attracts darkness. I know all about you. You should join me. With your dark magic abilities, we could have fun together."

"You're not my idea of a fun time. And there's nothing fun about what you're doing to Luna. It's time you left this place." I opened the ghost jar.

The room shook, sending picture frames crashing to the floor.

"Is everyone ready?" I lifted my chin.

My three familiars shot to the corners of the room.

I backed away into the empty corner, still holding the jar in front of me. We could do this. The ghost was weakening. Thanks to the magic artefacts placed in the room, his energy was draining and he'd soon be weak enough to capture and contain.

I couldn't have done this without my familiars. I'd missed not having a team to work with, who understood the power of magic and how incredible it was. I'd gotten so used to being alone and doing things my own way. I'd been wrong. But I could put things right. Capture this ghost, make Luna's apartment safe again, and she'd no longer be sick and fearful for her life.

That was step one. Then I needed to clear my name and make sure everyone knew Magda wasn't a dark witch. It was no small task, but I was up to it now I had my familiars.

The temperature zoomed from icy cold to blazing hot, making me sweat. Swirling black mist spun around the room as the ghost fought the magic containing it, slamming against the walls as he tried to break free.

"You're only making this harder on yourself. Come quietly. And if you behave, I may find you a nice quiet spot where you can't bother anyone else," I said.

"I don't want quiet. I crave destruction."

"You need to get a hobby, my friend. Have you tried puzzles? They're very soothing. Or how about bowls? It's good for working out your frustrations by smashing hard balls into one another."

"I'll destroy you all. I'll take your bones and grind them to dust. I'll—"

"I've had enough of this." I rushed forward and swiped the ghost jar through the mist.

There was an ear shattering scream and the dark mist evaporated.

I smacked down the lid and turned slowly, looking around the room.

"Is he gone?" Nugget said. "Did it work?"

A smile slowly crossed my face. "We did it. The atmosphere already feels different." I waved the jar containing the ghost in the air. "We got him."

Russell swooped around the room, squawking his delight. Hilda did her funny tap dance on the floor, and Nugget licked one paw.

I did a quick check of all the rooms. Everything was quiet, and there was a pleasing sense of calm. My magic was working again, and it felt amazing to use it for good.

"This deserves treats," I said as I returned to the living room. "Who's up for Chinese takeout?"

Nugget's head swiveled to the door. "Errr... what's that?"

221

I turned, my grin fading as my gut twisted. A thick red mist seeped under the door, bringing with it a foul sewer stench.

I looked at the ghost jar that held the ghost. "It can't be the same spirit. He's in here. I can feel his angry energy. We definitely got him."

"Then we have a problem," Nugget said. "Whatever that thing is, it feels like it wants to gut us and hang our entrails out the window."

The room darkened and grew stifling hot. The red mist swirled, growing larger. I saw a flash of fangs and claws as it morphed into a tornado.

"Everyone get back." I crowded my familiars behind me just as the red tornado engulfed us.

I grabbed Hilda before she was swept off her legs and tucked her inside my jacket. Russell was still flying in the air, but being dragged toward the center of the tornado.

I scooped him out of the air and tucked him in with Hilda.

Nugget caterwauled, his claws digging into the floor to stop himself from being dragged inside the swirling mass of evilness.

"Grab my arm. Hold on tight." I reached out my arm.

Nugget latched his claws into the fabric, but the tornado grew in strength. His claws ripped through my sleeve and slashed the back of my hand as he was torn away.

I grabbed for him, but I was a second too late. There was a roar, and a vicious face with fangs and glowing eyes appeared. It seized Nugget and ate him.

Chapter 20

Horror made me dizzy as I stared at the spot Nugget had been a few seconds ago. The ghost creature had... eaten him. I'd just got Nugget back, and he was gone again. Another of his lives taken because he was helping me.

"What's going on?" Hilda yelled from inside my jacket, her legs beating against my chest to get my attention.

I sucked in a breath. "That mist thing got Nugget."

The red tornado backed away, unpleasant chewing sounds coming from it.

I pressed a hand against my stomach. Of course, it was never going to be this easy. Luna was a powerful witch. If this was a simple haunting, she'd have dealt with the ghost on her own.

But what was inside the jar? Had I captured the wrong ghost again?

White hot anger flared inside me as a low rumble of laughter echoed around the room.

"Let Nugget go." I raised my hand and sparked magic.

There was more laughter. The tone was different to the first spirit I'd encountered. There must be more than one apparition haunting this place, and this one had been hiding until now.

"He was tasty. Thanks for my treat." The voice was low and female.

"Return him now, and I may spare you. You saw what we did to your companion. Don't think I won't do the same to you." I was bluffing. I'd only brought one ghost jar with me, but this spirit didn't need to know that.

There was another derisive laugh.

I growled in response. I was done playing nice with this spirit. I slammed magic into it.

The red mass wavered, but the laughter continued as if my magic did nothing more than tickle it.

I refused to retreat. Not this time. I had my team beside me, and we were more powerful together. And this ghost wasn't keeping Nugget.

"I could do with a hand out here." I opened my jacket and peered in at Russell and Hilda.

"We're ready. What do you need from us?" Hilda said.

"A distraction. But be careful. This thing bites!"

Russell zoomed out and over my head, sweeping around the mass and pecking at it.

The red mist reared up, making a grab for him, but he dodged and weaved, avoiding attempts to be captured.

"Don't get too close, Hilda. This thing seems hungry," I said.

"It won't want to eat me when it sees my full size."

I glanced at her. "Your full size?"

"Give me a magic boost, and you'll see what I mean. Touch my back and open your magic to me."

I kept a close eye on the spirit as I touched Hilda. I yelped and leaped back as she spasmed, her limbs lengthening, her body growing huge as hairy spines so sharp they'd cut through flesh sprouted from her.

"Holy broomsticks, Hilda! I had no idea you could do that."

"I couldn't until I was claimed as your familiar." She reared up, rubbing her fangs together, before lunging into the mist.

I was about to yell a warning, but given how terrifying Hilda looked, anything in her path would be wise to flee. Her monstrous size even sent a shudder down my spine, and I considered her a friend. More than that. She was my familiar. She was part of my family. And that meant I didn't want her getting hurt.

I waded into the fight, blasting magic at the mist as it circled us.

Russell was snapping his beak and raking his talons through the mist like a ninja warrior bird. Hilda was slashing with her fangs and hurling herself into the fight repeatedly, getting shoved back, but going right back in. I joined them, and we kept on fighting.

And I'd keep fighting until this was over. Magda's reputation had been ruined, as had mine, by things I hadn't been able to control. My life had felt over, but the truth was, it was just beginning. Now, I had a family again and a place that felt like home. There was no way I was giving that up.

"I'll kill you all," the enraged misty ghost roared.

"Do your worst. We're going nowhere. And leave my familiars alone." I slammed more magic into the ghost.

A hole appeared through the mist where I'd hit it.

Hilda scuttled back and thumped my leg with a hefty, hairy limb. "It's too strong. I can't find a way through its barriers."

"We're getting Nugget back. I'm not leaving him."

"How can we get to him? I've tried biting, punching, and magic. Nothing gets through for more than a second."

I stepped back. My power was beginning to drain. I'd need a time out to recharge soon, and this ghost wasn't showing any signs of slowing.

We were almost out of time and luck, and Nugget was still trapped inside this evil entity.

"Take me instead," I said. "Return Nugget and have me."

Hilda gasped, and Russell squawked and flew over my head.

The mass shimmered, before taking the form of a tall, slim woman.

"Is that what you really look like?" I peered at her features, but her face was shielded by a dark hood that was pulled forward so I couldn't get a good look at her.

"I take many forms. This is one I prefer." She drifted closer, her feet an inch above the floor. "You'd sacrifice yourself for the mangy creature I took?"

"Nugget's a friend. He's worth saving."

"You can't," Hilda said. "I feel the darkness this ghost gives out. It could kill you. Or... turn you dark again. We've just got you back."

Russell squawked in agreement and flapped his wings.

"I'm not going anywhere," I said. "This thing won't be able to hold me for long."

"You sound confident for a ruined witch no one believes in," the ghost said.

I stared at her. I knew that voice. I'd heard it somewhere before, but I couldn't place it.

I stood firm, my hands clenched. "Do we have a deal? Take me and give me back my fluffy familiar."

The ghost shimmered. "I could do with another meal."

"You didn't eat him. I know Nugget is still alive. And you're messing with powers you don't understand."

"I understand you well enough, Ash witch. You are nothing to be feared. You always were a broken family, and that was before you polluted yourself with Magda."

"What do you know about Magda and my family?"

"Come join me and I'll tell you more."

"Will you give Nugget back if I do?"

"I'll give you so much more than that rude little cat."

"Don't do it," Hilda said. "You can't trust it."

I didn't trust the ghost, but I couldn't see any other option. Nugget didn't deserve to be chewed up by this monster. And if anything bad happened to me, Hilda and Russell would have my back. They'd figure out a way to get me out.

The ghost wiggled its fingers. "Make your mind up, witch. I don't offer this to many magic users."

"Only the broken ones?"

She chuckled. "How perceptive you are. We're going to have fun together."

I grabbed her hand, wincing as an icy chill shot up my arm. The second we made contact, the world blotted black, and I vanished from the room.

The air tasted of smoke and cinder, and I blinked as my vision adjusted to the gloom. "Where's Nugget?"

The ghost's hand rested on my shoulder, and she turned me.

For a second, I saw nothing, then an image of the living room apartment appeared. Nugget was lying flat on his belly, covered in goo and snarling at the mist. Hilda and Russell stood beside him.

The fingers on my shoulder tightened, and the ice turned to fire as the ghost's grip dug into my flesh. A shudder of revulsion ran through me. It wouldn't be easy to get away from this strong, unstable spirit.

But I couldn't doubt myself. I had to remember Magda's teachings, and I had my new familiars waiting for me to return. Plus, Luna was relying on me. This ghost had to be punished, or my best friend would never recover.

"You should never have come back," the ghost purred in my ear.

"Why wouldn't I come back home?" I frowned as I lost sight of Nugget, Hilda, and Russell.

"Your old life was safer. No one bothered you. No one noticed you."

"Which was a problem. Ash witches need to be noticed."

"The only time you've ever stood out is for the wrong reasons. You gave yourself over to the darkness, just like your stepmom."

"What do you know about Magda?"

The ghost chuckled. "I watched her progress with interest when she married into the family. She was no match for the magic she became entangled with."

"Magda did that to save me. She was an amazing witch."

"She was as broken as you are. And Magda was arrogant. She thought she could contain a power far above her status. It ruined her the second she touched it. Just like it ruined you."

"You talk as if you knew her," I said. "Did you used to live in Witch Haven?"

"I've lived in many places."

"A straight answer would be great." I narrowed my eyes. "Are you the jerk who turned Magda into a murderer? Did you threaten to harm me so she had to go along with your plan?" I grabbed the ghost's hood, determined to see who she was, but she shoved me away, the imprints of her hands burning into my skin.

"That's no way to treat someone older and more powerful than you'll ever be."

"I have no idea how powerful you are. You can't be that strong if you refuse to show your face. It makes me think you're scared. If I know who you are, I'll be able to hunt you down and defeat you."

There was that annoying laugh again. "The Ash witch lineage is coming to an end. You're the last of them, and you're a bitter disappointment. It's a good job you have no relatives left to see your dismal performance. And with no heir to continue the line, it's the end of the Ash witches."

I scowled at her. I still had time to produce a few powerful witch babies. Sure, I needed a stable job, a place to live, and a guy to help that along, but it could happen.

"This sounds personal," I said. "What's the Ash witch coven ever done to you?"

"You've lived. That's enough."

The more I heard this ghost speak, the more I was convinced we'd met before. But I'd been distracted by her for long enough. It was time to get back to my familiars and Witch Haven.

I dug down deep into the well of magic I'd kept hidden for too long. It bloomed from my chest, down my legs, and made my toes tingle. I fisted my hands and slammed everything I had at the ghost.

She didn't flinch.

I gritted my teeth and tried again. This had to work. I refused to be this twisted ghost's plaything. Or her next meal.

The ghost raked a too long arm through the air, slamming into my stomach.

I flew through the air, the spark of pain in my gut making my eyes water. An oomph shot out of me as I hit the ground. I rolled onto my feet, then yelped as I was lifted and thrown about like a rag doll. Pain rippled through me, making me groan.

"You can be my puppet to control, or I'll stuff your hide and mount you on the wall. You'll be a fun addition to my collection of witch trophies."

That had to be a sick joke. I locked eyes on the dead, soulless face under the hood. The image instantly blurred.

"What have you got to hide?" I thrust my hand out, slamming magic straight into the ghost.

She dropped me and staggered back.

At last, I was getting through her defenses.

The ghost flew at me, her feet not touching the ground. Her hand wrapped around my throat and she squeezed.

I raked my hand through the spirit, trying to weaken her, but she was growing more solid by the second, taking my energy and feeding from my newly regenerated magic.

She growled in my face, and her clawed fingers tightened.

I scratched her hand as the air vanished and my lungs burned. My fingers brushed Magda's necklace and heat blasted out of me. The feeling was so familiar, yet shocking. The warmth bloomed through me, and a laugh shot from my lips. This was what true power felt like.

Holy broomsticks! I'd not used real magic for so long that I'd forgotten its primal, wild nature, and desire to play. My magic was back. And it was strong. So strong that it blasted out of me in an untamed pulse.

I laughed again. It felt amazing.

The ghost's grip vanished from around my neck and she retreated, her arms outstretched as if was warning me not to come any nearer. "What have you done? You were never this powerful."

I staggered to my feet as more magic pulsed out of me in hot waves. "If you hadn't tried to kill me, I'd still be the weak, broken witch I was when I arrived back in Witch Haven. I should thank you. Instead, I'm going to kill you."

"You can't kill me."

"I can. And I will." I spoke the banishment spell and aimed it at the ghost.

She dodged out of the way of the magic and spun through the air.

"There's no use running. I've got you." I fired out more magic.

"If you kill me, you'll never know the truth." Her words rushed out of her, her panic clear.

"About what?" It felt amazing to be back to full strength. How I'd missed being a real witch.

"Indigo! You know me. You recognized me the first time I made contact. You wouldn't kill a friend, would you?"

I hesitated. I did know this ghost, but she was no friend of mine. There was nothing but evil running through her veins, and she had to go. I inhaled, focusing on her banishment.

"Wait! I can tell you what happened the day you and Magda attacked the village." There was a quiver to the ghost's voice.

"I don't believe you. You'll say anything to stop from being slammed into oblivion."

"Listen to your instincts. I can be useful to you and rid you of that doubt you're full of. It's polluted you for too long. Keep me here, and I'll be your ally."

I lowered my hand. "Was it your fault? Did you turn Magda rogue?"

"No, but I know who did. And I'll tell you if you keep me alive."

"You're a ghost. You're already dead."

"If you banish me, I'll go to the empty place. I'll be alone."

"It's what you deserve."

She floated back and forth for several seconds. "I'll release your friend. I'll set her free."

"You'll do that, anyway. It's time you left this place. You have no right to harm Luna."

Snarling echoed around me as if a dozen wild beasts were about to attack. "Luna is more powerful than you realize. She isn't what she seems. Don't be too quick to trust her. A lot has changed in Witch Haven since you left."

"She's my friend. And I'm not afraid of you. You can't hurt me. Not anymore. You can't hurt anyone. Spirit, I demand you leave. You have no place here."

"Then you'll never know the truth. Are you prepared for that? You'll always have questions about that day. The day your life was ruined. I can help you. You'll find resolution if you let me live."

"You can't help me."

"I'll lead you to the people who turned you and your stepmom into killers."

I was tempted by her sly words. I longed to know the truth. Who'd targeted Magda? Were they pure evil, wanting to create a horde of servants to do their dark bidding? No one could be that dark. Or was it a direct attack on the family? The Ash witches had once been powerful, but by wiping us out and ruining our reputation, it meant there was no more power.

"Let me stay," the ghost whined. "I'll remain tied to Luna, but won't harm her anymore. She can be my anchor to the living world. I'll even give her back some energy. She'll be almost as good as new."

"You're not using my friend. She's not your battery to drain."

"I need a life source to live off. Or are you willing to sacrifice yourself for her, too? I'd take your energy gladly and let her go. My very own Ash witch. That would be entertaining."

"You're not using anyone. Not anymore." I slammed magic into the ghost repeatedly, blasting out spells and focusing on her banishment.

Her form vanished, sweeping around me in a cascade of foul-smelling mist, and more growls and snarls filled the air.

"Spirit, I banish you from this place. Release your hold on Luna Brimstone." I blasted out the incantation.

The ghost howled its displeasure before vanishing.

I dropped to my hands and knees, my body shuddering and my head spinning.

A second later, Hilda, Nugget, and Russell were in front of me and I was in Luna's apartment.

"You're back," Hilda said. "We lost you. The ghost caught hold of you, and you vanished. Where did you go?"

I sucked in a breath and rested back on my heels, so glad to be in familiar surroundings. "I'm not sure, but I don't want to go back there any time soon." I looked around the group. "Is everyone okay?"

Nugget curled around me and purred. "You did it. You got rid of the ghosts."

I shook my head. "No, we did it together."

Chapter 21

I closed my eyes and took a deep breath. It didn't feel like just two days ago I'd been battling malevolent spirits to save my friend.

My old house, no, my new home, was quiet. The rooms were cleared, and I'd even had some reclaimed furniture surreptitiously delivered from the local thrift store. It had taken some wrangling, but I was determined to be comfortable for as long as I stayed.

And I wanted to stay forever. The Magic Council was convinced the house had been obliterated, so they wouldn't come after me while I sheltered here.

It was a short-term solution, but it was the best I had right now. And that was good enough.

I opened my eyes and looked around. The atmosphere in the house was warm and inviting, and a mellow afternoon sun filtered through the window, lighting the dust motes that floated through the lemon scented air.

The peace was welcome. It was a different quiet to my old apartment. When I was there, I hid from the world. I'd used those walls to disappear behind and hadn't wanted anyone to know I existed.

I'd been holding my breath, terrified of drawing trouble to me.

Not here. The quiet was restful and embracing. I needed to figure out how to make this place my home permanently. Finally, after years of waiting, life felt good again.

A bang on the front door jumped me out of my silent revelry. I didn't answer it. There were only a few people who knew this place still existed, and they'd let themselves in, eventually.

As if on cue, the front door blasted open. Nugget strutted in, followed by Hilda and Russell.

Hilda dashed over and touched my foot. "We've got snacks."

Russell dumped a pile of still living worms on the floor and stepped back, looking pleased with himself.

I wrinkled my nose. "Good job, Russell. But I'm not in the mood for slime and mud today. How about we get takeout?"

Nugget hopped onto my lap, kneaded for a few seconds, then jumped up and curled around my shoulders. "I told him the worms were a lousy idea."

Hilda balanced on my foot. "He tried to bring down a cow, but it charged him, so he went for something more manageable." She patted Russell on the wing when he scolded her. "You did a great job. That cow was just in a bad mood. Any other time, you'd have got her."

"I'm sure you terrified that cow," I said.

Russell bobbed his head at me.

"He wanted to impress you," Hilda said. "But worms are full of nutrition, and you need feeding

237

up. Living off tinned peaches and takeout won't keep your magic healthy. And you don't want to lose it again."

I nodded. "I'm taking great care of myself, especially now I have three reasons to stay healthy."

Nugget purred and sniffed my ear, while Hilda and Russell bobbed around each other.

"What's the word on the street?" I said.

"Everyone's talking about Luna's miraculous recovery," Hilda said as she returned to my foot. "She's getting out of the hospital today."

I grinned and settled back in the seat, careful not to squash Nugget. "That's great news. We'll have to go and see her when she's out."

"There's also talk of an epic magic battle that went down in her apartment," Hilda said. "Your magic blasts didn't go unnoticed."

"I'm not surprised to hear that, but that's the least of our worries."

"What do we have to worry about?" Nugget said. "We got out of Luna's apartment without anyone noticing us. No one tracked us back here. And we're the only ones who know about the battle. That's how it needs to stay. No squawking to your buddies about this, Russell."

Russell ruffled his feathers and looked outraged, before gobbling down a worm.

"Olympus was also asking around about you," Hilda said. "Apparently, he wants a word."

I grimaced. "He can have several words. How about *I'm not here*. As long as I keep a low profile, Olympus won't poke around this place. Hopefully, he'll assume I slipped away in the dead of night." I had to hope that would happen, but in the pit of my stomach, I knew he'd be after me. Olympus wasn't a guy who let things go easily.

I looked at my perfect familiars. It felt amazing to live together again. I'd gotten Nugget some new towels, which sat in the corner of the room completely unloved. He occasionally went to his bedroom, but spent most of his time snoozing on the moldy bedding he was attached to. Hilda had some cotton wool to plush up her space under the cabinet, and I'd added new perches in each room, so Russell would have plenty of options for resting.

"Does this mean you're staying for good?" Hilda said. "You've fixed Luna's problem, so is there any reason for you to hang about?"

"Well... I mean, I could stay. I was thinking about it. And how will you all manage if I leave?"

"You do what you like." Nugget yawned in my ear. "We'll look after ourselves."

I leaned away from his fishy breath. "I don't want to leave, you fluffy jerk. Not anymore. And the ghost I banished made me curious. She knew Magda and the truth about why Magda turned dark and what happened the day we attacked the villagers."

"You can't believe that," Nugget said. "She'd have said anything to stop from being destroyed."

"I'm not so sure. And I knew her voice, but I couldn't place it. Maybe she had connections with Magda or an Ash witch. She could have come to the house when I was a child."

"You still got rid of her, even though she could have told you what really happened," Hilda said. "Weren't you curious?"

"I was, but I couldn't let her keep hurting people. She had to be banished. Now she's gone, and the other ghost is contained, so the knowledge is lost."

"Not necessarily. We could always release the other ghost and interrogate him," Nugget said.

I glanced at the sealed ghost jar on top of the magic cabinet. "I don't want to let that thing out again. And right now, we have more immediate issues to deal with."

"Like food," Nugget said.

I grinned. "I was thinking that we needed to find a way to clear Magda's name."

"How are you going to do that?" Nugget said.

"I have her journals. That's a start. I'm going to look through the rest of them. Magda could have hidden more information inside the pages that I've yet to discover. I may even be able to identify the witch who manipulated her. Once I've done that, I can send the information anonymously to the Magic Council so they'll investigate the case again and clear Magda and me of any wrongdoing."

"They won't do that. They've already closed the case because it's been solved. They think you're trouble," Nugget said.

"Then we'll have to show then they're wrong."

"You could always ask Olympus for help," Hilda said.

"No way. He's not a friend. He'll arrest me if he knows I'm still in Witch Haven."

"He's not a friend yet, but he could be. And those piercing dark eyes are always welcome here."

I laughed. "Do you have a crush on Olympus?"

"Don't you?" Hilda said.

"Nope. He's too arrogant, and he runs the Magic Council. He's responsible for the pain I went through."

"Is that really true?" Hilda said. "He didn't pass your sentence."

"Okay, it's not entirely true, but I don't see how we can make him an ally."

"We could start by not making him an enemy," Hilda said. "Offer him useful information. He could warm to you if you make an effort with him."

"I'll think about that." Dealing with the spiky, dangerous Olympus Duke wasn't going on my to-do list anytime soon. "But that leads me to our next problem. We have to find a way to get the Magic Council to agree this house can stay."

"And convince them concealing the house was the right thing to do," Hilda said.

"Good luck with that," Nugget said. "The Magic Council hate being taken for fools. I don't know why. It happens to them often enough."

"At least I'm blameless," I said. "I can say hand on heart I had nothing to do with this deception."

Nugget snorted. "You're going to throw us to the Magic Council?"

"You can't do that. We protected all the beautiful things in this house," Hilda said.

Russell blasted round the room, squawking his unhappiness.

I laughed. "Okay, I'll save your hides by not letting on what you did, but we can only hide behind the magic wards for so long. Eventually, someone will spot us coming and going and report their suspicions to the Magic Council. We have few friends in this village."

"We can show them all the magic in this house is only ever used for good," Hilda said. "They'd be wrong to destroy so much power, especially if it's used for their benefit."

"They've been wrong plenty of times before," Nugget said. "It doesn't stop them from continuing to make mistakes."

I nodded. "Which is why we need to tread carefully. The Magic Council isn't on our side. Until they soften to us, we have to be discreet, or I'll go back to prison and you'll all be on the street again."

"So no more blowing up ghosts in the center of the village," Nugget said. "Shame, I enjoyed that task."

"I bet you didn't enjoy all the goo stuck to your fur when the ghost spat you out," I said.

"I'm still finding it in crevices it shouldn't be in," he said.

I glanced at my hands. A faint white glow shimmered on my palms. "And I need to figure out what to do with all this new power, before I blow myself up and take all of you with me."

"It is freaky," Hilda said. "It doesn't feel like your power."

"I don't think it is all mine." I brushed my fingers over the amethyst necklace that had saved me from the ghost. I wasn't sure whose power I was channeling, but it would take a while to get it under control.

"You don't want the Magic Council seeing you tangling with powers beyond your ability," Nugget said. "Or that'll be a one-way ticket back to prison."

"I sure don't. I'll find a way to get this magic under control. It'll just take me some time."

"I don't know why you're worrying about all this. These are small problems. We can easily fix them," Nugget said.

"They are? They seem pretty huge to me. Who injected you with a blast of positivity?"

"I did. I'm my own cheerleader. And we make an awesome team. We banished the ghost, Luna's apartment was saved, and she's getting out of the hospital. And I don't have to live on outdoor scraps, anymore."

I loved having the old Nugget back, even if he came with a side order of sass.

I petted his head. "We'll sneak out and see Luna later when she's back home." I couldn't wait to have my old friend back in my life.

But once everything was settled, I'd have to work out my next move. If I was keeping this house, I needed paid work, but had no clue where to begin with that. How could I find a job when I had to be on the lookout for the Magic Council?

"Someone's outside," Nugget said.

I tensed in my seat. "Is it Olympus?"

Hilda scuttled over to the window. She looked out, then raced back and jumped on my hand. "It's Luna's uncle."

"What's he doing here?" I stood and headed to the window. Albert was stumbling around, shaking his head and looking at the rubble.

243

K.E. O'CONNOR

"He must be looking for you," Nugget said.

"Something's wrong with him." I rushed to the door, Nugget still wrapped around my shoulders, and pulled it open. Hilda and Russell were right behind me.

I waited until Albert's back was turned and then stepped through the magic. I didn't want to give him a shock by appearing out of thin air.

"Hey, are you looking for me?" I said.

Albert jumped as he turned, his eyes wide. "Oh, yes! Indigo, I'm so glad you're still here. I didn't know this had happened to your house."

I nodded and tried to look as forlorn as possible. "The Magic Council decided to get rid of it. They didn't think it was safe."

He swiped a hand down his face. "I'm sorry to hear that. I always thought this was a beautiful house."

"Same here. Is something wrong?"

Albert looked around, his gaze frantic. "Possibly. I was hoping she'd be here."

"Who are you talking about?"

"Luna! She should be in the hospital recovering."

"She checked herself out?" I said.

Albert shook his head. "It's the strangest thing. I'm trying not to panic, but she seems to have vanished."

I walked over and grabbed his shoulder. He was shaking. "Tell me what happened to her."

"Luna's been doing so well. She started to recover two nights ago." His gaze flashed to my face. "Did you have something to do with what happened in her apartment? I know you said you were going to help. I got to take a look inside yesterday and it was

244

a mess, but the ghost had gone. It felt like a safe place again."

"I did. And I'm glad Luna's getting better. She won't be bothered by those ghosts anymore."

"There was more than one?"

I nodded. "There were two spirits attached to her apartment. I trapped one and banished the other."

He puffed out a breath. "I appreciate your help. Luna does, too. She's been asking about you and hoping you'd come to see her."

"I was thinking the same thing. But I'm confused. Why do you think she's vanished?"

"I went to get a coffee, and when I came back, Luna was gone from her room. I waited around for a while, but she didn't return. I told the doctor, and he looked for her. I had a horrible feeling something was wrong. When I looked around the room, things had been knocked over and the bedding disturbed, as if she'd been dragged from it."

"You think someone abducted Luna from the hospital?" I glanced back at the house. It couldn't be the ghosts. I'd dealt with them.

"Maybe. I don't know what to do. I've reported it to the Magic Council, but they don't believe it's a missing person case. They said she's an adult and can discharge herself from the hospital if she wants to. They told me to wait seventy-two hours to see if she turns up. I can't wait that long. She's vulnerable. What if something bad has happened to her?" His chin wobbled. "Are you certain you got rid of those ghosts? They haven't come back?"

I hesitated. I assumed I'd banished the female ghost, but if she hadn't been destroyed and had somehow recovered, she was vengeful enough to go after Luna.

"Indigo, you have to help me. I don't know what's happened to Luna. The Magic Council isn't interested, and I'm losing my mind with worry. She could be anywhere. She could be scared or in pain. I need to have her back. Luna is the only family I've got left."

I grimaced at the sharp reminder about my involvement in his loss.

This should be over. I thought everything was back to normal, but it looked like I was wrong. It felt like it was only getting started and there were more dark times to come. Would I get through them?

I glanced at my familiars, and they all nodded at me.

I rested a hand on Albert's shoulder. "Whatever it takes, I'll get Luna back for you."

He staggered into my arms, his forehead resting against my shoulder next to Nugget. "I'm sorry I called you an evil witch. You're not. You were an amazing friend to Luna. You looked out for her. I... I just need her back."

"And you'll get her back." I gave him a hug, while Nugget licked his head.

I looked at my familiar surroundings. I was back home and Witch Haven needed me. My adventures were just getting going, and they wouldn't end until everyone I cared about was safe.

About Author

K.E. O'Connor (Karen) is a mystery author living in the beautiful British countryside. She loves all things mystery, animals, and cake.

If you want to be part of the Witch Haven crew, practice spells, solve a few murders, spend time with amazing witches and their talking familiars, and get a **free** book, join her weekly newsletter.

Every Thursday you'll get news on the mysterious happenings in K.E. O'Connor's world.

Sign up today.

Newsletter:
https://BookHip.com/QKGDWJW
Website:
www.keoconnor.com/writing
Facebook:
www.facebook.com/keoconnorauthor

Also By

Spells and Spooks
Hexes and Haunts
Curses and Corpses
Muffins and Moonlight
Cupcakes and Cauldrons
Pancakes and Potions
Hauntings and High Jinx
Hauntings and Havoc
Hauntings and Hoaxes
The Case of the Screaming Skull
The Case of the Poisoned Pumpkin
The Case of the Cursed Candy
Fire Fang
Silvaria

If you enjoyed

Spells and Spooks

turn the page to read an extract from the next Witch
Haven mystery

HEXES AND HAUNTS
ISBN: 978-1-915378-29-3

Chapter 1

Is it possible to kill someone with a cupcake? As I eyed the desserts in front of me with suspicion, I figured it most definitely was.

"Those are the worst cakes I've ever seen. It looks like you've squashed a gnome and covered it in ghost goo." Nugget, my cat familiar, was perched on top of a kitchen cabinet, looking down at me with disdain on his furry face.

I frowned at the misshapen, sunken cupcakes covered in gray icing. "How did I get a simple baking spell so wrong? I can't give these to Albert to sell in the bakery. His customers will think he's trying to poison them."

My spider familiar, Hilda, ran up my leg and tapped the back of my hand with one hairy limb. "It's the effort that counts. He'll appreciate them."

"That's not true in this case," Nugget said. "You can't take those things to the bakery. You'll give Albert a heart attack, and he's stressed out enough as it is."

"I'm trying to be helpful. I don't know why I bothered." I picked up the tray of a dozen ugly cupcakes and walked to the trash.

Russell, my other familiar, soared over my head, flapping his wings and cawing unhappily.

"You can't want to eat these," I said to him.

He settled on the countertop and bobbed his head.

I set down the cupcakes. They definitely weren't something anyone in their right mind would buy, but they probably tasted okay. And I didn't mind gray icing, so long as I closed my eyes and didn't think of ghost slime.

I glanced at the cauldron bubbling on the stove. It would be ten more minutes before the location spell was at full strength. That gave me enough time to have a quick cup of coffee and try my baking.

I switched on the kettle and pulled out a mug and a tub of instant coffee.

"You're really going to eat one of those monstrosities?" Nugget said.

"We all are. After all, you're my familiars. It's your job to protect me from anything potentially deadly."

"I'm not protecting you from your own terrible baking," Nugget said.

Russell bobbed nearer to the cakes, an eager look in his beady black eyes.

"Russell loves my baking, don't you?" I stroked his silky black wings.

"He's only interested in them because he thinks they look like giant toads," Nugget said.

"My cakes don't look like..." When I squinted my eyes, they did sort of look like misshapen

251

amphibians. "Okay, so baking spells aren't my forte. I'm still getting the hang of all this extra power." I lifted my hands and admired the sparkle shifting across the surface of my palms.

It had only been a few days since I'd reacquired my full witch powers, and a little extra boost, and I was adjusting. And as the cakes demonstrated, my adjustment wasn't going so well.

I pulled out a plate and set a cupcake on it.

We all looked at it. No one made the first move to take a bite.

I grabbed a knife and cut it into four pieces. "Let's do this together."

"Count me out," Nugget said. "I don't want to get sick."

"I'll try some," Hilda said, from her favorite position on my shoulder.

"My cakes can't be any worse than eating all those flies you love so much," I said.

"Flies are delicious," Hilda said. "You can't beat them. But I'll try a bit of cake now and again. How about you, Russell?"

Russell hopped from foot to foot.

I lifted a piece of cupcake up to Nugget, but he wrinkled his nose and hissed at me.

"You need to work on your familiar skills," I said to him. "Hilda and Russell have gotten into the swing of it."

He stood, turned in a circle and settled back down so he was looking at the wall.

I grinned, despite his crabby behavior. I still felt lucky Nugget, Hilda, and Russell had accepted me as their witch. After abandoning them for more than a decade, they had every right to turn their beaks and noses up at me and find someone else to support in her witching duties. But they'd stuck by my side and helped me in times of trouble. I'd be eternally grateful to them. Although I wouldn't be baking them any thank you cakes anytime soon.

I made my coffee, took a few sips, then lifted a piece of cupcake. I took a bite. It tasted of... nothing. It didn't taste sweet or sour. It was just bland. I swallowed the cake.

Everyone was looking at me as if they expected me to keel over and foam at the mouth.

"It wasn't that bad," I said. "Go on, you two, you haven't tried your pieces yet."

Russell grabbed his cake and swallowed it in one go.

Hilda scuttled onto the counter and took a tiny bite of cupcake.

A few seconds later, Russell heaved up a soggy lump of cake. He shook out his wings and backed away.

"Oh dear! Was it really that terrible?" I said.

He cawed mournfully, before flapping up to his perch in the corner of the kitchen.

Hilda backed away from the rest of the cake. "Hmmm, the trash is the best place for them. Let's forget about the baking. We can help Albert much more by finding Luna."

I pointed at the cauldron. "That's what the spell is for. I needed a distraction whilst it was maturing, otherwise I'd have kept tinkering."

My best friend, Luna Brimstone, had been taken from her hospital bed while recovering from an attack by a malevolent ghost. I'd promised her Uncle Albert that I'd get her back, especially since I'd aggravated the ghost who most likely took her. But so far, I'd had no luck. This location spell was my latest attempt at finding out where Luna was.

With a sigh of regret, I tossed the cakes into the trash, then headed to the large oak kitchen table where I'd laid out a huge map of the local area.

The village of Witch Haven was a small place, home to six hundred and sixty-six magic users. That number always stayed the same. Although it had temporarily changed when I was seventeen, and was seduced by dark magic, alongside my wonderful stepmom, Magda. We'd wiped out ten percent of the population in a single day.

I tried not to dwell on that too much. It wasn't my finest hour.

I studied the map of the village. The house I lived in was set along a quiet dirt track, close to the forest. It was a perfect, secluded location for a witch in hiding. And that was definitely my tag. Although I was working on changing that.

And one step to doing so, was to find my missing best friend and prove to the Magic Council I was no longer a black magic using witch, and had a positive reason for being in the village.

"Check to see if the spell is ready." Hilda was perched on my shoulder again.

I walked over and gave the liquid a stir. It shimmered from orange to green. That was a sign the ingredients had mixed and the locator spell was active.

I used a small ladle to decant the spell and headed back to the map.

Russell hopped onto the table from his perch and stood to one side of the map. Nugget shuffled around to watch, then yawned and closed his eyes. I knew he was interested in what was going on, he just pretended not to care.

I used a pipette to extract some of the spell and held it over the map. I took a deep breath and attempted to channel my power. The troubling factor in this spell casting game of chance was that it wasn't entirely my own power I was using, so the channeling wasn't always spot on.

Before my stepmom had died, she'd left behind a number of magically charged items in this house. I was wearing her amethyst necklace, which supercharged my own ability to such an extent that I often sparked magic without even realizing what I was doing.

I raised one hand, closed my eyes, and centered myself. I imagined Luna, her warm, mischievous smile and the way she always greeted me with a bone crunching hug.

I was blessed to still have her as my best friend. Even after everything that had gone down, she was steadfast and loyal. And she was the first to come find me when I returned to Witch Haven under a cloud of darkness.

Now it was my turn to help her.

I dispensed three drops of the spell onto the map. I opened my eyes and watched as they rolled onto the paper like tiny pearls. Rather than sinking into the map, they shifted around, seeking out my missing friend.

When the spell worked, the three drops would merge on the spot where Luna could be found.

After ten minutes of waiting and watching, the drops of liquid stopped in opposite corners of the map.

"Are you sure you mixed the ingredients right?" Nugget said.

"Positive. You all watched me do it," I said.

"This is a good sign," Hilda said. "If Luna was dead, the liquid wouldn't have moved at all."

"Or it would have sunk into the graveyard," Nugget said.

The liquid hovered, as if it was about to move, but was uncertain where to go.

"It's showing you Luna's not anywhere," Hilda said.

"That can't be right. She must be somewhere. A witch doesn't just vanish without a trace."

We were all quiet as we continued to stare at the map.

"She could have been taken into a limbo-like place," Hilda said. "The place ghosts lurk when they have nothing better to do."

"I get stuck there each time I die," Nugget said. "It's not that much fun."

I grimaced. He was still reminding me of the time I'd accidentally buried him when I thought he'd died. Nugget was magically charged, so could regenerate if ever something fatal happened to him. He was a cat with not just nine lives, but potentially an infinite number of lives, thanks to Magda's magic that kept him alive.

"You can't take a living person into limbo," I said.

"Luna could be unconscious," Hilda said. "That would give her a foot between two worlds. The ghost who has her—"

"If it's even that mean ghost from her apartment," I said. "We still haven't figured out who took her for certain."

"Yes, but if it is that ghost, he's powerful. We barely survived when we went up against him. He could be holding her there. And it seems logical it would be him. Who else would want to harm Luna? She's a sweetie."

I threw my hands up in frustration. A blast of magic shot out of one palm and smashed a hole straight through the ceiling. I ducked as plaster rained down on me.

I lowered my hands and stared at them. "Sorry, house. I still don't know my own strength."

The kitchen door slammed in response. It wasn't only the residents of Witch Haven who had magic. This amazing house was a little special, too. And it didn't like it when I blasted a hole through important things like ceilings.

I hurried out of the kitchen and dashed upstairs to assess the damage. The magic had not only blasted through the floor, it had also gone through the roof. I could see daylight through the not insignificant hole.

I stopped by the window and looked outside. My eyes widened, and I grabbed the window ledge.

Olympus Duke, Head of the Magic Council, stood by the pile of rubble next to my house.

Nugget hopped onto the window ledge and growled. "He's still not leaving us alone. He's been back every day since you escaped."

"He can't know this house is still here," I whispered. "The magic wards are keeping it concealed."

"Olympus is a strong magic user." Hilda ran up my leg. "Maybe he can sense the wards, but can't figure out where the magic is coming from."

"Or he can sense you," Nugget said. "Especially if you keep smashing magic through the roof of a hidden house. We won't stay hidden for long if you keep misfiring your spells."

I wrinkled my nose. The Magic Council wanted me for lots of reasons. I owed them money, and I'd escaped their custody after being arrested for the illegal use of magic. Plus, I was hiding in a house they thought they'd destroyed. They had plans to turn me into a shadow and remove my magic. But there was no way I was letting that happen. My life was getting back on track, and I wasn't having it torn away because the Magic Council couldn't see sense. Witches could change. I was living proof.

And if that wasn't enough of a problem, I had to get Luna back. I owed it to her. And I owed it to her uncle. If the Magic Council got in my way, things would turn nasty. But my friend's safety meant the world to me. If getting her back put the Magic Council's pompous noses out of joint, then so be it. I'd deal with the consequences when they finally caught up with me.

"We need to give the Magic Council something else to worry about," I said. "Surely, I can't be the only witch they're interested in. There must be some other badly behaving magic user out there they can target."

"I've got a plan to deal with Olympus and his minions." Nugget hopped off the window ledge.

"What are you going to do?" I asked.

"I've been meaning to try out some diversion magic. There are a few spells I've been studying in Magda's books. They could be fun to use on Olympus."

"What kind of diversions are we talking about?" I said. "You don't want the Magic Council chasing you, too."

"If they do, I can escape them. I'm fast on my furry paws. A few spells cast around the village will keep them busy, and they'll forget all about you." Nugget bounded down the stairs before I had a chance to stop him and learn more.

I looked at Hilda. "Why's he suddenly being so helpful?"

"Because even though he doesn't like to tell you, he's happy you're back and have decided to stay. He was miserable with no witch to claim as his own."

I smiled to myself. I could get used to this life. I'd only been back in Witch Haven a short time, but it already felt like home again, and I was planning on staying put. So long as I could prevent the Magic Council from stripping me of my witch abilities. Oh yes, and get rid of my debts, figure out a way to keep this house, and locate my missing best friend.

I spotted Nugget out the window, scurrying away in the opposite direction to Olympus.

Olympus didn't see him. Instead, he knelt and placed something on the ground before leaving.

"What's he up to?" I muttered. Anything the Magic Council left for me to find was never going to be good. The last time he visited, he'd brought a list of debts I needed to repay.

"Send Russell out to get it," Hilda said. "He's fast on the wing. If anyone is watching, they'll just see a black blur zoom past."

I headed back down the stairs with her and directed Russell out the front door to grab whatever Olympus had left behind.

He sped back a moment later with a piece of rolled paper gripped between his talons.

I extracted it and unrolled it. It had a single sentence on it. We need to talk.

My gut clenched, and I shook my head. How did he know I was here? Everyone believed the house was gone, so why was he coming back and leaving messages for me to find?

"This could be a positive thing," Hilda said. "Olympus is softening toward you. And we need him as an ally."

"Olympus Duke won't ever be my ally. He was the one who arrested me and locked me away almost as soon as I returned to Witch Haven."

"Maybe Albert has put in a good word for you," Hilda said. "He must have told Olympus you've been helping to find Luna. And you did banish those ghosts from her apartment."

"I banished one." I gestured at the ghost jar containing the trapped ghost that sat on Magda's magic cabinet. "But I let the other go. No, I can't trust Olympus. We don't need him involved with this. He'll only interfere. And there's no way the Head of the Magic Council will bend the rules, and that's what we need to do to get Luna back."

I headed back into the kitchen, finished my coffee, and then tried the location spell three more times. I got exactly the same results. The liquid zoomed around the map for several minutes, before the three separate drops hovered in the corners.

I dispersed the spell and rolled up the map. "We need to try something else. There must be a spell to show me where Luna is."

A thudding on the front door made me jump.

Russell squawked and flew out of the kitchen.

Hilda clung to my shoulder. "That sounds like someone is in a bad mood. If they keep thumping so hard, they'll knock down the door," she whispered.

"It doesn't sound friendly. But how has that someone found the front door to bang on in the first place?" I crept toward the door and peered cautiously through a window beside it.

Ursa Wyrm stood outside, her lips pressed together as she clasped a squirming Nugget...

Hexes and Haunts is available in e-book and paperback.

ISBN: 978-1-915378-29-3